UNDERNEATH THE MASK

DES SWEET

Editor: Jasmine Acena

Alpha Reader: Megan Henry

Cover Model: Joshua Bely

Images: Font and background licensed from Canva

contents

content warning

The content of this book is not suitable for all readers. It includes adult themes and situations that may make some uncomfortable. Possible triggers include:

Violence: torture, knife violence

Criminal Activities

Dark Themes

Stalking

Dubious Activities

Non Con/ Dub Con / CNC

Unhinged Gifts

Manipulation

Explicit Sexual Content

DEDICATION

Mask's Kinks

Stalking

Voyeurism

Subs

Dirty Talk

Dub Con Non Con

Blood Play

Gift Giving

Amanda's Kinks

Masked Men
Dark Romances
Praise
Dirty Books
Doms
Knife Play
CNC
Degradation

PART ONE

DAYS UNTIL
HALLOWEEN

MASTERPIECE

CHAPTER ONE

Mask

I have a secret. I could find her anywhere—not because I know everything about her, but losing her would never be an option. This game I've started of cat and mouse is the only way we can be together forever.

A rustling sound awakens the paved abyss as the wind blows dry, crunchy leaves around the half empty parking lot, rolling them across the cool pavement and down the street. When the leaves settle and silence falls over the dimly lit, dusk-washed streets again, I hear her. *I'm so fucking obsessed.* My sweet, rainy little storm cloud trudges out of the hospital entrance and to the light rail stop. *The way my fingers ache to brush over her soft, creamy skin is unbearable. They would recognize her any place; ravishing every part of her. I imagine the slender curve of her neck beneath my hand. It's elegant and sleek, sloping gracefully into her dainty shoulders, sprinkled in tattoos.* I'm painting a scene in my mind, creating a wild fantasy. *Her breasts would heave and fall beneath me as I lean over her body, memorizing her beautiful face. Everything about her is pure perfection: she's my little masterpiece.*

The bell rings, signaling the train is about to arrive. It rips my attention away from her for just the slightest moment. I hate this part of our route home. I quicken my pace, hanging back just enough to be one of the last people to board, leaving me seated in the very front with my back to her. It doesn't bother me nearly as much now as it used to. Once I realized I could use the mirrors all over to see her, it made losing sight of her for only a few moments bearable. The second warning bell sounds and I step onto the light rail train seconds before the entrance doors slam closed behind me. As I slide into my seat, I pull my baseball cap down lower over my face and tug on the hoodie strings of my black zip-up sweatshirt. It takes me less than a minute to locate where she's sitting. I count the number of seconds, racing my best time.

It's a short ride to her stop. When we arrive I climb off first, slipping away into the shadows to watch from my hiding spot. She should be going to the gym tonight. Like a creature of habit, my little muse turns up the street that leads to the shops nestled inside the neighborhood, a secret sanctuary for its inhabitants. I follow her, unfazed by my own behavior. We've been doing this little song and dance for a few weeks now, moving as one: hunter and prey. I sneak along behind her, ducking down the side streets and alleys every time she looks back over her shoulder. She's uncomfortable, but it doesn't stop me from studying the way she moves, committing it to memory. It's not always safe to go walking through the streets of the city alone at night. I'm also searching, taking in every aspect of our surroundings, like a vigilante.

The long summer days have faded into eerie, dusk steeped nights as fall's impending reign steals the last bits of sunlight from the sky. *If I'm going to keep her safe from the dangers of this world, then I can't let her out of my sight.* Our evenings together are something I've come to look forward to. She works out at the gym for an hour after long shifts at the hospital, and I sit across the street watching her inside while eating a different flavor of ice cream. The way she bends and moves should be a sin. I have to adjust myself so no one else can see the intoxicating spell her body has me under. The sweat glistening on top of her skin does unspeakable things to my thoughts. Mesmerized, I allow my imagination to run wild as I watch her rhythmic movements. *If only I could run my hands all over her body, the way they crave to touch her. My body pinning hers against the wall, burning with desire as I drag my greedy fingers over her soft, dainty curves.* Just the thought has me itching to race across the street and act on my impulses. Instead, I take a deep breath and shove another bite of ice cream into my mouth, licking the spoon clean. *Soon,* checking the time on my watch, *but not tonight.* Not yet. Our game has only just begun. I intend to play with her a while longer, savoring the minutes I plan to spend with her from now until Halloween. The smile creeping across my lips is sinister. It's so hard to contain my excitement. I've plotted out all my moves in this diabolical game of chess. I continue to watch her, enthralled with the object of my attention as I shove bite after delicious creamy bite into my mouth.

Soon my ice cream is gone, and she's wiping down with a towel. I watch with longing as she tucks it into her gym bag. Lifting her water bottle, my masterpiece parts her plump seductive lips, and takes a long swig. I imagine they are parted around my dick as she swallows it inch by inch until she's gagging and unable to breathe. I snicker to myself. She doesn't even realize the danger she's in at all times. I'm a goddamn masochist when it comes to her.

As she emerges from the gym, I watch and my body tenses with the instinctive rush of adrenaline urging me to follow her. I stand, moving slowly, naturally, so as not to draw any unwanted attention to myself. Once she's goldiloxed in front of me, I return to the shadows, stalking her. Disguised by the darkness, I slink behind her, diligently following her onward to the next destination. Home. I can't wait. My favorite part is watching her undress from the alley at night. My dick throbs hard and warm against my leg as I imagine her naked. I reach down to stroke my cock, uncaring if anyone sees. She's mine. I'll do whatever the fuck I want when we're together.

The dark tendrils of night snake around both of us. We're almost home and all alone; just my masterpiece and me.

She stops unexpectedly up ahead, and I duck behind a car parallel parked on the street. Cautiously, I peer out from the cover of the car. She's not looking back at me. She's looking down the alley where she stands. Her foot slides back, preparing for fight or flight. The moment it does, I slip from my hiding spot, walking as quickly as I can without giving myself away. Her chest rises and falls in slow motion. She's paralyzed with fear. I kick a rock from one of the well-manicured yards next to the sidewalk. The noise startles her, and she takes off in a sprint. *That's my girl. Run.*

It's probably just a neighborhood cat that spooked her or a strange shadow. Despite that, it's still necessary for me to figure it out. I like to make sure I'm certain my masterpiece remains unscathed by others. I turn down the alley with a loud skid as my shoes slide over the loose gravel. Ahead of me, the moonlight reveals a shadowy figure slipping away in the other direction. I follow after them at a jog, intent on figuring out just exactly what they think they're doing following my trophy.

I stalk my target closely, taking extra care to remain undetected until I decide to reveal myself. We've covered an entire block and are nearing the halfway point of a second when a dog barks from behind me. There's nowhere to hide and no sense in appearing guilty of following them.

The figure in front of me turns just as a flash of lightning strikes in the overcast sky. Thunder cracks, warning us both of the impending fall storm. Soon the rain will turn to sleet, then snow. I keep my head down to conceal my identity. When I look up, he's turned back around and is continuing his trek. I slow my pace, adding extra seconds to every stride I take. We're both shrouded in darkness, with two street lights between us. Now I'm walking more like a potential victim, and less like an actual threat. Hopefully, I get lucky and they're stupid enough to take the bait I'm using to lure them right into my trap. Everything about my body language changes. I'm about to pass across the alley my target disappeared into. In about thirty goddamn seconds, I'm going to show them exactly why it's not okay to creep on another man's personal belongings. My masterpiece was created for my eyes and my eyes only.

I reach into my hoodie and pull out the mask from the pocket. I've been carrying it around just in case I wanted to kick things up a notch, but now it seems pretty useful for keeping my face hidden. I slip it on, hiding behind the purple neon glow of the dark threads, and count down in my head. *Five. Four. Three. Two. One,*

My new target's fist lands against my forearm. The block catches him off-guard and he stumbles back like a scared little kitten. Good. He wasn't expecting me to try to take the upper hand. I use the opportune moment to slip my hand around his neck, lifting him in the air, then slamming him to the cement ground with a thunk. The imposter stalker tries to climb to his feet, but my foot delivers a powerful kick into his ribs so hard I swear I felt some of them snap.

"It's not a good idea to stand up right now. I enjoy beating the fuck out of bullshit strangers," I say, slamming my elbow into his back. He collapses at my feet with a groan.

"That's my good little low-life criminal. Stay down. Kiss my feet." I growl.

"What kind of kinky shit are you into?" He asks, his voice cracking.

I chuckle, not giving him the satisfaction of an answer, and he stays low. The imposter lays there belly side down against the cool cement, not even bothering to strain and get up.

I kick him again. "I said, kiss my fucking feet, asshole."

Deciding that I might be a little more crazy than he is, my new little play toy lifts his head and kisses my black cross trainers. Once he lays back down, I compliment him.

"That's better," I say, leaning down to grab him by the hair.

He's forced to look at me while I'm free to hide behind my mask. "I don't give a fuck about anything else you want to do in this neighborhood, except for one thing." I pause dramatically, relishing in the delightful way the power trip rolls through me.

"If I ever catch you so much as thinking about looking at my girl, let alone near her, I will fucking kill you. I'll snap your neck without thinking twice. Are we clear?"

The dumbass has the audacity to answer. "But isn't that basically saying I shouldn't be in your neighborhood at all and that if you catch me, you'll kill me?"

I release him, clapping my hands in an agonizingly slow round of applause for him. "I guess you aren't as stupid as I expected you to be."

He says nothing, simply glaring at me with his lips twisted into a sneer.

"Should I assume your silence means we have a mutual understanding?" I snap.

More silence. He's really starting to piss me off, so I slam his face into the concrete without warning.

"What the fuck was that for?" He complains once he recovers.

"You were annoying me. I asked a question, and you failed to answer." I reply.

"This is the last time I'm going to ask. Have I been clear? Do you understand what will happen if I ever see you again?"

1

---

1. *Goldiloxed- To be the perfect amount. Not too hot, and not too cold. To be just right.*

Admired

Chapter Two

Amanda

I'm paralyzed with fear, stopped dead in my tracks and standing smack dab in the middle of the alley. Everything about me is enticing and vulnerable. The perfect victim, all alone in the dark, and still a block from the safety of home. Although, my audience doesn't know that yet. My brain tries desperately to reason with my frozen body. *Run, Amanda. We can make it. We have to get somewhere safe.* My muscles groan in response, protesting my brain's commands. *We are losing precious seconds.* This time when I try to take a step forward, my legs shake like jello. They don't have time to malfunction. A rock skids across the concrete behind me with a loud scrape. Out of the corner of my eye, a shape springs to life, and so do my feet. They carry me swiftly across the shadow streaked sidewalk, toward the safety of home. I don't stop until I'm clambering up the front steps and through the heavy mahogany door. My hand slides over the cool metal lock, turning the tumbler over behind me. I take a deep breath and scramble across the dark hallway into the kitchen. The French doors leading out to the wood deck are locked and the blinds are drawn closed. I don't dare turn on any lights. If they know where I live, or if they followed me home, whoever they are—I don't want them to know that I'm here. Alone. I slip across the smooth wood planks on the kitchen floor. My fingers land against the cool marble countertops and slide a few inches lower to pull the drawer handle open. I don't risk a glance down into the knife drawer without a quick sweep over the dimly lit kitchen. Certain I am safe and alone, I look down in search of the largest knife I can find. My eyes scan the contents of the drawer frantically as my fingers carefully rummage through it. They are just about to wrap around a gleaming silver handle when the lights flip on above me. I clutch the knife greedily, jump, then spin around, letting out a high-pitched scream in hopes someone might hear me.

"Hey, I'm sorry I scared you. It's just me. I came home early. Christ, Amanda, I think you screamed so loud the neighbors are going to come over and ask if everything is okay." My boyfriend says, as he crosses the room to comfort me.

"Jesus. Fuck. Goddamnit, you scared me," I confess, my heart still thundering in my chest and my fingers wrapped around the knife so tightly, my knuckles are turning white.

Feeling self conscious and stupid, I set the knife down slowly on the countertop as I breathe a sigh of relief. Before I can do anything else, he's pulling me protectively into his embrace. "What has you so jumpy and worked up?" He asks me as he drags his thumb across my jaw, then plants a tender kiss against my forehead. His lips calming all of my nerves, that burn like fire, screeching, we are still in danger.

I close my eyes, leaning into him, inhaling deeply. His spicy warm sandalwood and leather scent washes over my senses, calming me instantly as my racing heartbeat slows. His warm, buttery voice is rasping in my ear as he apologizes. "I didn't mean to freak you out. I was upstairs, working on reviewing the security setup for the art gallery show later this month, and I thought I heard the front door slam. I assumed the wind caught the door. Before I came downstairs to get dinner started, I turned the shower on for you." He runs his big, strong hands over my arms.

I stutter for a moment, struggling to find the words I need. "I think someone was following me." My confession leaves my eyes brimming with tears as the reality sets in.

"Did you see someone?" He asks, suddenly even more serious, a look of concern contorting his face.

"Not exactly." I reply. "I heard a sound down the alley, and I saw a giant human-shaped shadow."

"A giant shadow?" He questions, quipping his brow at me.

"I know it sounds unbelievable, right?" I say, feeling childish.

"No, baby. I believe you, but you know it probably was just an animal or the wind blowing stuff around. If it will make you feel better and you'll let me, I can pick you up and drive you home from now on." He offers in a reassuring tone.

"No, you're probably right, but what if it wasn't?" I ask, looking up into his eyes, searching for some sort of reassurance.

"Let's do this. We can call the police. I'm sure they will send an officer out to poke around. I'll call it in and you can go grab a shower while we wait. Try to relax while I cook. You know their response time for something like this might be a little on the long side, but I think it will help you feel better. You have the next two days off. Skip the volunteer hours at the clinic tomorrow and get some extra rest. They will be just fine without you this week."

I can't help it. Something about the way he rationalizes the entire situation makes me feel at ease. He's right, though, my hours have been taking a toll on me and the clinic will function just fine without me tomorrow. I shiver. I know it's from the adrenaline, and my body decompressing, but my sweet boyfriend mistakes my reaction for having an actual chill.

"Go on. You're shivering, Amanda. Next time call me, or charge a ride to my account. I don't need you walking home, covered in sweat from the gym all the time, and catching a cold." He gives me one more big bear hug. Kisses my cheek and says, "Take your time and when you come back down, I'll have a nice big bowl of soup waiting for you."

He places the knife back in the drawer, shaking his head. "This isn't the kind of knife you cut vegetables with. You stay out of my cutlery and I'll keep supporting your reading habit. Good deal?"

I crack a smile at him. The warmth of a nice hot shower is more than appealing. After all, it was probably nothing more than an alley cat getting into the trash. *It was much too large to be a cat. It was a man. Don't be stupid.* The intrusive thoughts in my head push back against the false narrative I'm using to mask my true emotions. Fear pulses its way through my body once more, gripping my thoughts and forcing me to picture the shadow covered dark outline of a man's body.

I glance over my shoulder at my perfect boyfriend. He's laying out vegetables for chopping and slicing. Deciding to take his advice, I slink off to the shower with all the best intentions of relaxation.

In the shower, I try not to think about everything that happened on my way home tonight. I probably shouldn't have agreed to calling the police. It feels silly to have gotten so worked up. The warm water runs over my face and I breathe in the steam. Droplets beat down on my skin in a soothing rhythm as I close my eyes, allowing the water to melt my anxiety away. This is exactly what I needed after a long day at work. I shut the water off and grab my towel. In my closet I pull a comfy pair of sweatpants from the drawer and rip an oversized Halloween-themed T-shirt from a hanger. When I'm dressed, I check to make sure my reading tablet is charged and eye the stack of paperbacks on the nightstand. I could spend tomorrow curled up with something from my pile.

Walking back down the stairs, I already feel better. There are voices coming from the entryway and I realize midway down there are two police officers standing in the foyer.

"Hey, are you Amanda?" The older officer with speckled gray hair and a mustache asks when he notices me on the stairs.

I nod my head, unable to speak for a moment as I process the situation.

"Your boyfriend was just telling us you think someone followed you on your way home tonight. Did you get a good look at them, and can you give us a description?" He questions.

"Um," I stammer. "It was pretty dark and there were a lot of shadows in the alley."

"Hey, that's okay," the other officer chimes in. "There's been a pretty recent uptick in crime. It might not be a bad idea to pick up some pepper spray or re-evaluate your transportation plans," he suggests, trying his best to be helpful.

I nod.

"Well, without a lot of details, unfortunately, there's not much we can do. We will drive through the alleys and watch for any suspicious behavior. Call us back if it happens again."

"I understand, officers." I thank them politely and then scurry past off to the kitchen.

In the kitchen, as promised there's a giant pot of chicken noodle soup simmering on the stove. I take a deep inhale before grabbing two bowls from the cupboard. On the counter is freshly sliced bread. I sigh. He's a great guy. I really am lucky to have him. I just wish we were more compatible in the bedroom. But what he lacks for being vanilla, he more than makes up for when it comes to caring for me. As I spoon us each a bowl of soup, I overhear one of the officer's voices carry through the hallway. I pause, straining to hear what exactly he's saying.

"You should look into a camera system, sir. A lot of your neighbors have them. You can pick them up for around a few hundred dollars and pay for live monitoring, or just casually monitor them yourself from an app on your phone. If someone is following your girlfriend home, you can bet a camera system will pick it up. Talk to your neighbors and ask around. Maybe someone caught something on video tonight. If anything turns up, call us back. Otherwise, have a good night, and really the best way to prevent crimes like this is to keep the situation from happening to begin with. If you can pick her up from work or she can carpool with a friend, it really would be a much safer choice now that it's getting dark earlier." I hear the door open, then close.

When he comes into the kitchen, he offers me a sympathetic smile. "I'm sorry. They weren't overly helpful." He chuckles. "But, Amanda, seriously think about letting me just give you a ride. You heard them. It's not safe."

I stare him down, refusing to give up control of my freedom to get myself to and from work. "They said crime was up. What else is new? Crime always increases this time of year. We live in a decent area and most of our neighbors have cameras."

"Is that what you heard?" He asks, rolling his eyes. "Honestly, just quit your job and then you wouldn't have to worry about any of it. I've told you I make more than enough money to take care of both of us." He wraps his arms around me in a light embrace.

I take my bowl of soup and a slice of bread, then sulk my way to a chair at the island. Not this again. My mother and him both have made it clear they want me to settle down, get married, and start popping out babies. Working gives me a sense of purpose. Neither one of them understands what it's like to save lives. I sigh, slurping up my dinner. We eat at the island in silence. He tinkers with work stuff on his tablet and I'm happy to read on my phone.

Right as I finish, he's scooping the bowl from in front of me and leans in for a kiss on my cheek. "I'm sorry. I'm selfish."

"It's okay," I mumble, appreciating his apology. It's not like he did anything wrong. All he's trying to do is protect me.

"I just could never live without you, Amanda. You don't understand how much I love you. Everything about you is amazing, and I know I could never love anyone but you."

His confession catches me off-guard, but I lean into it. Standing up from my chair, I wrap my arms around him and go in for a kiss. His lips brush mine softly. He's always so goddamn gentle, as if he's terrified of hurting me. I kiss him harder and he pulls back.

"Come on, I'll tuck you in. I still have some work to finish up, but you should get some rest." He whispers against my lips.

My mood instantly deflates. I don't want to rest. I was hoping we could have sex, but I guess this is just him protecting me and trying to be a good guy. I shouldn't say that. He is a good guy. I'm just not used to being taken care of like this. It's like he's never interested in being intimate anymore. I'm not sure what's going on between us. It feels like we are both trapped in a sexless roommate stage with our relationship, and it leaves me questioning where things are headed. Then he tells me to quit my job. This man is so confusing. Despite my mixed emotions, I help him clean up and then we trudge upstairs together. He's going to work all night and I guess that means one handed reading for me. I still have needs and if he's not going to take care of them, then I'll take care of them myself.

MASK

Chapter Three

Mask

Under the cover of the alley, I lean against the corner of her detached garage. The shadows cast an added layer of darkness over everything. We're separated by only a small courtyard where the patio furniture glows beneath small bursts of lightning. It's been storming off and on all night, filling the air with the wet, musty smell of damp leaves. I'm all alone just waiting for my muse to appear in her window. My thoughts are consumed with concern over the imposter we encountered on our way home tonight.

She's mine. No one else is allowed to follow her like that. Her body is for my eyes only, and this fucker just had to ruin the little game I was playing. I'm only giving him that one warning. If I catch anyone following my girl again, I'll fucking kill them. I don't care if it's the same person or not. I check the time on my watch, feeling my jaw tick impatiently. Any moment now, the show will begin. My cock twitches with excitement, the anticipation making my thoughts run wild, imagining the things I can only watch from my secret hiding spot.

Finally, the light flips on in her bedroom and I watch greedily as she waltzes into the room. My eyes follow her, knowing exactly where she will wander. They track her every movement, savoring each moment. She has no idea I'm watching, which only makes my heart beat faster, and my dick grow harder. I almost want her to catch me. The thrill of it consumes me as I imagine she invites me up to her bedroom and forces me to act out the pages of her books together, allowing me to finish her off at exactly the same time the words do. I can almost hear her in my fantasy, begging me to fill her with my cock. Realizing I've become distracted, I shake my head. I have to stop myself if I want to come at the same time she does.

My focus snaps back to Amanda. She's on a mission to select the perfect book to crawl into bed with. My sweet siren stands in front of the pile of books, wearing nothing but a robe that is much too small for her. The edges of the hem just barely sweep across the round curve of her ass cheeks. When she walks it bounces across her sun-kissed skin, giving me glimpses of more.

Her book pile is where I got the idea for the mask, which came in handy earlier tonight. It was from a book she read a few weeks ago. When I looked it up to read, I found out it involves a masked villain. He made stalking his victim his entire personality. After I read it, I knew it was perfect. The main character and I have so much in common.

I bite my lip and moan softly, rubbing my hand just briefly across my stiff cock. Watching her is a god damn treat, and I can't help but to indulge. She eventually makes her selection, then settles into bed. It's only a matter of time before she's reaching down between her legs to touch herself and her neglected pussy. *It's been over a month since the last time*—I stop myself from finishing the thought.

My hand slides beneath the waistband of my sweatpants, gripping my throbbing dick, desperate for relief. I stroke myself softly at first, denying the pleasure of a firmer grasp. Each time my fingers roll over the barbell of my piercing, I suck in my breath and stifle a moan. I keep the same rhythm as Amanda as she dips her fingers between her folds and drags them over herself. She pauses for a moment, reaching into her bedside table to retrieve a toy. I watch on eagerly, still stroking my shaft as pre-cum leaks out from my excitement.

The way she runs the vibrating silicone over her clit has me aching to be inside of her. I'm rock-hard from my front-row seat to her super secret pleasure hour. My tongue wets my jealous lips as she caresses all her favorite spots, building her orgasm until she gets to the end of the scene in her book. I continue to match her speed, enjoying the way my own orgasm is building. I watch greedily, all the while wishing it was my tongue bringing her this level of pleasure. My mouth salivates at the mere thought of tasting her sweet juices upon my hungry lips. *Soon it will be my tongue.* Patience, not yet. Not until we know for certain the imposter is no longer a threat, not until I've had my fun. She's always had a taste for the dangerous, the forbidden—I'm just giving her what she's always wanted. I know deep down she's going to love everything I have planned for the two of us.

My breath falls faster and heavier. She's getting close, and so am I. I've been watching her for almost half an hour. It's so fucking hypnotic: the way her tempting little pussy captivates my every thought. I've waited so long to feel her throbbing around me, drenching me in her cum. I imagine that's exactly what is happening while we are caught up in the moment acting out the scene.

My cock aches for relief as she explodes all over her toy. I want nothing more than to be her favorite play thing right now. Jealousy and relief flood my body as I allow my orgasm to rush over me, cum pulsating out of my dick and shooting all over the cement at my feet.

In the bedroom, the glow from the light clicks off. She's going to sleep. This is my cue to leave. There's nothing more to see tonight.

MINE

Chapter Four

Mask

It's been days since our secret meeting and I can't get the fantasy of my beautiful little masterpiece, choking on me, out of my mind. I'm tempted to act it out with her. Night after night I've followed her home, all the while my cock demanding the sweet torment of her lips around it, desperate for the sensation of their embrace. Tonight is no different. Except it is. Amanda is leaving her shift several hours late. It was a busy night in the emergency room. We ride the light rail together. She's unaware of my presence, despite how empty the train car is. Me, on the other hand, I haven't taken my eyes off of her in the mirror. This night is an anomaly. There's not a single part of it that feels ordinary. I drag my fingers over my face in frustration as I try to convince myself the nagging feeling in my gut is wrong.

When we exit the light rail at our stop, I catalog every suspicious person we encounter, every noise, every shadow. Our ride is always too short for my liking. It only gives me a few minutes to calm my mind, then we are on the move again. I can sense a strange shift in the air. Something doesn't feel right. It's the first time in days I've felt like we aren't alone. Maybe it's because the night is so much darker now, or maybe it's because we aren't alone.

Good girl. I think as she skips the turn to the gym, heading right for home. Like the professional stalker I've become, I hang back for a few minutes, hoping if we aren't alone, they'll get excited and make the first move. I watch Amanda walk away from me and it's agony not being able to stare with my full attention as she does. Instead, I wait until she's just barely out of my watchful gaze. My legs are itching to follow her, but I count her steps in my mind to the beat of her gait, mentally cataloging her location. Just as I'm about to step from the shadows and slink after her ahead of me, I catch an all too familiar shadow slide in behind my girl.

Game on, asshole. I slip from my hiding spot, walking briskly to clear the space between us as I place the mask on my face. A sinister smile spreads from ear to ear as I gain on the imposter who dares to test my mercy. The smartest thing to do would have been to disappear, but now I have no choice.

I should have recognized a psychopath when I met one. Of course when I set my boundary, I made her even more desirable. This is all my fault, and now I have to clean up my mess. It's a good thing I've concocted a contingency plan for every possible scenario. I smirk, my face concealed. *Checkmate, little fucker,* I think, seething with anger as I clench my bone white fists.

I trail the object of my obsession aggressively, thinking about all the ways I can take the imposter out. Mess with my belongings: pay with your soul.

We've only walked a few hundred feet with me hot on his heels. My fingers wrap around the cold metal blade of my butterfly knife, securing it in my pocket. Its dangerous edges will slice into the imposter's rib cage smoothly, carving between them, turning his body into a Jack-o'-lantern. My fingers tremble anxiously as I flip the knife from one hand to the other, attempting to distract them from their impulsive desires. I can't wait to sink my blade deep into his vulnerable flesh over and over until he is no longer a threat to my perfect little masterpiece.

How dare he return to play with my favorite toy. His biggest mistake was coming back for more. He's either reckless or delusional if he thought our little chat the other day meant I wanted to share.

My finger rubs the handle of the knife again. It's not my fault he failed to heed my warning. If only he'd stayed far away from Amanda. Then none of this would even need to be happening. Amanda and I could have continued on playing our little role play like a pair of star-crossed lovers performing with the streets as our stage.

I'm working myself into an irrational frenzy. Something inside of me snaps and I charge the imposter from behind, muttering, "Fuck it."

The knife glistens in the moonlight, an ominous omen of the deadly damage I intend to do with it. I slam into him right as he turns to look back over his shoulder. The knife cuts into him effortlessly, like butter sinking deep between his ribs. His eyes bulge as his voice pierces the quiet streets around us, crying out in agony. Before he can recover from the first incision, I stab into his torso a second time. I didn't expect stabbing him would be this easy. The rush of adrenaline is exhilarating and thrilling. I'm riding a high, already thinking about the next rush. Ahead of us, Amanda has spun around to watch on in horror as I remove the pest from our game like an exterminator eliminating a pesky rodent. Once she unfreezes and I've stabbed Mr. I-Should-Have-Minded-My-Own-Business another time, Amanda's feet finally take flight. She bolts up the nearby alley, taking her chances in the dark because what I just subjected her to was probably a little traumatizing, but it's just the kind of thing she should be into. I only want to keep her safe. There's no telling what the soon to be dead guy was going to do to her if I hadn't been here to intervene. She should honestly thank me. *I think I know just how she can show me her appreciation for keeping her safe tonight.* My cock aches at the thought of taking her for the first time—

Smack! The guy I'm supposed to be murdering lands another punch to my jaw. This time, my head snaps back from the force. He underestimates my skills. I'm a trained killer; very fucking dangerous. I tsk, taunting him, goading his pride into lashing out stupidly. He falls right into my trap, taking the bait like a moth to a flame. Obsessed with escaping me. Every ounce of his energy is rerouted to the monumental task of evading my clutches and surviving long enough to make it to the hospital. Judging from the heavy blood loss, I would wager his chances of survival are slim if he doesn't succeed before I get another slice in. His lunge provides the perfect opportunity to cut into him again. He reaches out to try to choke me, but his hand runs down my bare chest as it slips beneath my zip-up hoodie. I shove him from me easily, watching with a satisfied smirk beneath my mask as he falls to the ground, gasping. There's no way he's going to survive, so I stab him a few more times, then carve a gang tag into the side of his neck all the while he meagerly tries to fight me off. When I've finished, I wipe the blade on the bottom of my jacket then leave him for dead in the gutters. The department is swamped. They'll cut corners on this one, especially if they think it's gang-related. By the time they find the body, I'll have already permanently erased and replaced the footage, erasing my footprint completely from the area. Walking swiftly, I take off down the alley, looking for any clues that my sweet masterpiece has been on the same route. From what I can tell, I'm banking on her going to the gym, even if it means running in the opposite direction from home. I grin beneath the mask, jogging to the gym.

I make it to the bottom of the street just in time to see her frantically keying in the after-hours access code to the door, and bolting inside.

This couldn't be more opportunistic. It's like the universe is begging me to take advantage of this opportunity. I've been thinking about her perfectly taunt, pretty lips wrapped around my cock all week and what I'd give to feel her neglected pussy wrapped around my cock while I slide it in and out of her slick, wet opening. My heart is racing as I slink up the block to the gym door. I key in her access code effortlessly. What kind of stalker would I be if I didn't know her code? My cock flexes in agreement as I think about everything I'm going to do when I find her. I can't fucking wait.

DEPRAVED

Chapter Five

Amanda

My finger fumbles, typing the entry code in wrong the first time. In a panic I look back over my shoulder and swear I can see the neon glow of his mask down the street. My hands shake uncontrollably as my breathing quickens. It's so hard to think clearly, but I will myself to take a shallow inhale, then release my breath slowly, focusing only on the numbers and keying them in correctly. *5-2-8-0.* The lock clicks and I ease the door open, then slip inside stealthily. I'm careful not to disturb the bells that hang on the door. Once the lock clicks closed, relief floods my senses, but only for a moment. I need to find somewhere to hide. The question is, where? My eyes skim the gym, frantically searching for a solution. The first spot they land on is the bathrooms, and I shudder at the thought of hiding in a dirty public restroom. Maybe as a last resort, but I continue searching for a better option moving through the dark gym, anxiety pumping through my veins. I hope to hell he doesn't find a way in. The only option is to prepare for the worst. There's an all too familiar nagging in my gut, and I know I will regret ignoring it if I do.

I scan the gym. There's literally no good place to hide. Time is also not on my side. Judging from how far down the street he was, if he somehow managed to see me slip in here, then there's a really good chance I only have a few minutes remaining before he comes bursting through the door. *Fuck, why didn't I just request a ride?* I am seriously regretting being so stubborn. If I would have just let my smothering, celibate boyfriend take care of me, none of this would be happening. *Why am I like this?* I think with a shiver.

Everything inside of the gym is dark and motionless, as if frozen in time. It's rare I find myself here so late and at such odd hours of the day. The corners of the room are shrouded in shadows, tempting me to seek shelter in them, but even if I do, their inky tendrils are no match for electricity.

If he turns on the lights, there are even fewer places to hide. *I have to keep moving. I can't just stand here out in the open. Hide, Amanda. Just fucking hide.* I wander near the locker rooms considering whether or not I can climb inside of a locker and then quickly decide against it, remembering all the stupid ideas in the slasher movies. Maybe I can lay down at the end of the row of treadmills. That way I can at least try to run. *Try to run. This is pathetic, Amanda. What are you doing?* I sigh in frustration. The treadmills aren't big enough to hide me, but the rowers might work if I need somewhere to hide in a pinch. I'm running out of time. My eyes dart around frantically looking for other options and then they land on the open-concept yoga and barre studio. There's a supply closet. The key is hanging next to it. I dash across the gym in a hurry and debate slipping inside with the key, but decide it might look more suspicious. As I slip inside of the supply closet, I freeze.

The bells on the entrance door jingle and my body tenses. Someone else is in the gym. Who am I kidding? I know exactly who else is in the gym. I'm no longer alone, trapped in the same building as my masked stalker. The smart thing to do would have been to go out the back alley door and run home. Fuck. *Why didn't I think of that sooner?* I ease the door closed softly and panic.

There are shelves full of yoga mats on the bottom row and it just might work to build a yoga mat fort to hide behind. I drop to my hands and knees getting to work. Hopefully their tight, rubbery rolls will conceal me. Once I've constructed the best hiding space possible, I lay down on the shelf, motionlessly. All I can do now is wait and hope more people arrive soon, but it's the dead of night and the reality is no one else is going to come. The seconds tick by, slowly turning to agonizing minutes, until it feels as if an hour at least has passed. I want to breathe with relief, to silently celebrate my success in outsmarting the masked man from earlier. A shudder courses through my body. The way he just stabbed the man on the sidewalk behind me. It could have been me. It was so close to being me. I'm getting myself all worked up again. The tears burn in my eyes, threatening to spill out and down my cheeks like hot rivers of regret staining my skin.

Jesus, I promise I'll stop reading slasher romances, stalker books, and I won't stream any of my favorite Halloween movies this year. I'll give it all up cold turkey, I think to myself, utterly distraught, and desperate to make it home alive.

The door jiggles and I'm once again frozen. *Please, just don't come in here.* The door creaks open and my jaw drops. *Fuck.* He's coming in here. I watch, horrified, as he takes one long stride into the supply room. *There's no way I can make it past him and slip out of the shelf unnoticed.* I think, sizing up his figure, unable to see clearly in the dark.

He fills the entire doorway in a predator's stance, his body language raw, dangerous, and alluring. It reminds me of the men from the pages of my books, masks and all. I shouldn't be attracted to him, but I can't help it. His presence is intoxicating. It floods my senses with a wild mixture of fear and arousal. Despite being absolutely terrified of what's going to happen next, I find myself fantasizing and unmistakingly turned on by the thought of him plunging his swollen cock deep inside of my aching pussy. My needy little cunt craves the sensation of being stuffed full of a throbbing, hard cock. It's been weeks—maybe even a full month or more—since the last time my boyfriend touched me like that, and yet he's just as protective and affectionate as always. I bite my bottom lip, squeezing my thighs together tightly, enjoying the momentary relief the pressure provides .

Snap out of it! I scold myself, blinking several times to clear the glazed over dryness. Once my vision clears, I realize his shadow cloaked figure no longer fills the doorway. My eyes dart across the room, frantically searching for movement. Finally, I spot his neon threads glowing on the other side of the supply closet. He's looking at the screen of his phone and there's a blinking dot that can only be me. He takes a step to the right and checks the screen. *Has he been following me?* My lips open and close, not making a noise as I choke on my silent scream. He slips his phone in his pocket and starts pulling things off the shelves and racks. When he comes up empty-handed, he turns to face the shelf where I am hiding. Through the yoga mat turned telescope, I can see splatters of blood on his shoes. The sight of the blood makes me woozy and lightheaded, but not because I'm not used to seeing it. *That blood could have easily been mine.* Shit, my blood could still end up on his shoes tonight and the thought of it has me breathing heavily as I succumb to a panic attack. I cover my mouth with my hand, focusing on small sips of air from my shallow breathing at first before switching to a slower, more meditative pattern. All I can think about is trying not to move and hoping I've made myself small enough to be overlooked. *I should have locked myself in with the key.* The regret rushes through my thoughts. *This is bad, so bad. And what the actual fuck was wrong with me for fantasizing about him a few minutes ago?* Even now, my pussy is humming with desire as I contemplate all the wrong decisions I made tonight. Intrusive thoughts flash through my head as I imagine him finding me. Above me, he's clearing the shelves. I'm running out of luck, I realize as I gulp down a wave of terror. I want to slam my eyes shut and disappear: to somehow make a grand escape. At this point, I'm desperate enough to try anything. I close my eyes and count backwards from ten, but when I open them, I'm greeted by the fluorescent glow of his neon eyes staring right at me from his perfect view of everything on the bottom shelf. I gulp, swallowing the lump forming in my throat. *Fuck!*

***

"There you are, Amanda," his voice is a menacing, low, deep rumble. I'm captivated, but only for a minute, before my ears realize he's using something to distort his voice, as if he's afraid I might recognize it. "What a naughty girl you are hiding like a little moth: drawn to the darkness, and unable to escape me."

The blood rushes through my ears, and I open then close my mouth to respond, but no sound comes out. I want to scream. *What good would that do when there's nobody around to hear it?* I want to run but his large form towers over me, filling all the space between us with his shadows. I don't stand a chance against him. Maybe I can persuade him not to murder me by enticing him with something else. My pussy throbs, guiltily starved for the sensation of being stretched out and filled. Realizing I'm just staring at him and before anything else can happen, his hand wraps around my ankle. He gives one hard tug and I come flying off the shelf, right into his waiting arms. I should be fucking frightened. My nipples bud in response, hardening while he holds me pressed against his wide, muscular chest. It's impossible to control my thoughts. I'm enjoying this all too much and it's sickening, but I can't stop. His body radiates heat in a way I didn't realize it would. Every nerve inside me has erupted with pleasure. He feels dangerous: it's fucking irresistible.

"So nice running into you here tonight, completely unplanned, and all alone," he croons, tormenting me as the depraved depths of my cunt clench, trying to contain the juices leaking out inviting his cock to take me in exchange for my life. Even if he doesn't let me live, fulfilling some of my fantasies might just be enough to help me come to terms with dying. I mean, on the plus side, I would die a satisfied woman.

I say nothing once more. It feels as if every inch of me is plastered to him: savoring the calm, even way his chest rises and falls.

His fingertips dance their way down my jaw until he's tipping my head up to stare at the glowing threads. "My, my, my, Amanda. What's a stunning woman like you doing out all alone like this?" He tsks.

I get the feeling he's not waiting for an answer as he continues reprimanding me.

"You're lucky I've been watching you. That man was planning to hurt you, but I couldn't let him do that to you, Amanda." He rasps.

A small nervous squeak escapes my lips. *He's been watching me. How long?* I wonder.

"Don't be scared, Amanda. I'm not here to hurt you. I only want to be rewarded. You see, I have these thoughts about you and I just can't get them out of my head." Every word that leaves his mouth is dripping with danger.

Is he saying what I think he's saying? Excitement pulses through me, and I'm genuinely curious about what he has in mind. But only for a moment. Trying hard to be brave, I whisper, "What is it you want from me?"

Even though his embrace is warm and inviting, I tremble in his arms. Fear grips every nerve in my body. He gives a satisfied huff, gloating at having trapped me into asking.

"I'm so glad you inquired," he says, snatching a strand of my hair from my ponytail and giving it a twirl around his index finger before smelling it.

When I yank my head away from him, he releases the hair, catching me instead by the base of my ponytail and pulling my neck into an exposed position. I hold my breath, unable to move if I wanted to. It's harrowing as bone chilling second after second ticks by. Until finally, a finger brushes across the tender soft skin on my neck. His rough skin tickles enough to tempt me into closing my eyes and making this psycho happy. Then I can run home to safety.

It's almost as if he can sense my brain buzzing back to life and plotting an escape. In an attempt to steal my thundering heart's attention back to him, he growls in a deep, rumbly throaty voice, "I want to fuck those pretty lips and then feel your wet little cunt wrapped around me."

I become as rigid as the victim I am, trapped in my predator's firm grasp. He controls my every move. He controls my fate; whether I live or meet the same fate as the man he killed for following me. I can tell he's waiting for a response.

"Yes," I whisper.

"Mmmmm." I can feel his chest vibrate against me with his satisfied moan. "I was hoping you'd put up more of a fight, but I suppose willing participation can be appreciated. Let's just pretend, for now, that you need a little more motivation."

Just like that, he shoves me back and pulls a knife from his pocket. He drags me after him from the supply closet and out onto the main floor.

"I love an audience, but I don't want any interruptions." He says, steering us to the posing room. He flips the sign on the door over to **In Use,** then pulls us inside.

"I can't wait to watch you. Maybe you've noticed. It's a hobby of mine." The masked man rumbles before he closes the door and locks it.

The room is dark, except the ominous glow from his neon mask. Above us track lighting runs across the ceiling for maximum control. One wall of the room is covered in mirrors. My reflection stares back at me and I look away, ashamed of what I'm about to do.

"Undress." He commands.

I grip the edges of my hoodie to pull it over my head, but his words make me pause.

"Stop," he demands.

"What?" I ask, my brows furrowing together.

"What do you say?" He replies, holding his hand up to his ear.

I roll my eyes, annoyed but still too terrified to complain. I decide to cooperate since it gives me the best chance of survival.

"What do you want me to call you?" I ask, not wanting to spend any more time than I have to with my masked captor.

"Hmmm." He sighs, thinking it over.

"Call me Mask Daddy," he growls.

I giggle, unable to stop the laughter from springing forth and erupting to fill the room with its sound. He says nothing. *Oh fuck, he's serious.* I think to myself and then clear my throat.

"Yes, Mask Daddy," I say as seriously as I can before I rip off my hoodies and strip out of my clothes until I am standing in front of him, completely naked.

SIN

Chapter Six

Mask

She's a fucking masterpiece, crafted in sin: every curve on her body a forbidden desire. She stands in front of the mirrors, where I can see nothing but her perfect reflection. I can't wait to feel the squeeze of her hotness while she comes all over me. I snap my fingers at her and wave the knife around.

"You're going to be a good little whore tonight, aren't you, Amanda?" I ask, pointing it at her.

She shakes her head yes.

"Use your words."

"Yes, Mask Daddy."

The sound of her voice has me relishing in the way it rolls off her tongue. I've waited so long for this moment.

My eyes roam her body, tracing every line and committing it to memory. I dip my free hand beneath my waistband to stroke my cock a few times.

"Be a good girl and get on your knees, Amanda. I'm going to fuck those pretty lips of yours and if you so much as think about biting me—" I let my words trail off.

She swallows hard and doesn't say a word as I clear the space between us. I tower over her, pulling my cock free with one hand and holding the knife against her collarbone with the other. Her lips part open, inviting me to slide my dick inside. She takes inch after inch of me; her gagging, an erotic symphony of beauty composed entirely for me. Her tongue glides over my barbell, sending a rush of pleasure through me. If I didn't know any better, I'd say she's enjoying this. To my surprise, her hand slides over mine to grip my cock, allowing me to grab her ponytail, tugging lightly at first and then harder as I deepen my thrusts. I'm picking up speed. She's gasping for air as I watch in the mirror. Her eyes are wide and watery staring past me in her reflection. A moan rises in my throat in response as her throat closes around me with every pass in and out of her lips.

"That's it, Amanda, such a good little slut. Now swallow every last drop." I shoot my cum down her throat and feel her gag. More leaks out and she gags a second time. "Mmmmm. I hope your pussy feels as good as your mouth."

In the mirror, I watch as I pull my cock slowly out from between her swollen lips. It's drenched in saliva and cum. I release my hold on her ponytail; dragging my hand over her neck, allowing my fingers to grip it tightly for a moment before wandering down her chest and over the swell of her breasts to tease her nipples. Her back arches and her head falls back, popping my cock all the way free.

"Bend over on all fours and face the mirror. You're going to watch me fuck you," I command.

She does as I say while continuing to suck in air as she drops to her hands, shuffling around to face the mirrors. Then she looks at me in it and says in a sultry tone, "Yes, Mask Daddy."

My eyes stare at her glistening pussy, obsessed. She's right here in front of me, and all mine for the taking. Approaching her from behind, I lean over her, gripping my masterpiece by her hair once more. I tap the blade of my knife against her neck and lift it over her shoulder, and down her back before folding it up and putting it in the end of my shoe, where I can grab it quickly if I need to. Before I release her hair, I rasp in her ear. "Are you ready to watch me fuck you, Amanda?"

"Yes, Mask Daddy."

"Mmmm, that's my girl, Amanda. You know how to get me hard." I release her hair, then drop to my knees. Taking my position behind her and running my greedy hands over her hips and around to cup each one of her toned, firm ass cheeks. Running my hands inside her thighs has my cock begging to slip inside her. Not yet though. My hands have an agenda of their own as each one of my fingers swipes through her folds to stroke her clit. She fights back a moan. "What's wrong? Does my touch bring you more pleasure than your toys? How long has it been since a man pleasured you, Amanda?" I ask.

My thumb and pointer finger slide together to stroke her slick hot clit. She quivers from my touch, still fighting back her moans. Her head drops and I tsk her. "Look up, little slut. I told you I want you to watch me fuck you so that when you close your eyes, it's the only thing you see."

She bites her lip uncomfortably, but returns her gaze to the mirror. I run my fingers over her another time. She's ready. Her pussy is nice and wet, just waiting to take every inch of my dick.

"You're falling apart for me, Amanda," I growl, placing the tip of my dick against her entrance. "You've never looked more stunning."

I slide my head in slowly, watching it disappear into her as she gasps and then a moan finally escapes her lips when my barbell slips into her pussy. "That's right, little slut. Moan for me. I like to know that you're enjoying it as much as I am."

My cock is more than halfway in when she adjusts herself, widening her stance and dipping her hips in order to take more of me. I reach around to rub her hard throbbing clit, running my finger over it just as I feel her take the last inch. "Look at you, all this perfection, just waiting to be wrecked by me. You've got me buried. How does it feel to know I'm all the way inside of you, Amanda?" I ask.

"Good," she moans.

It excites me so much, I thrust my hips into her. "That's my girl, cum for me," I groan right before hot liquid oozes from her core and around me until it's leaking out of her and onto the ground. It's so fucking hot it has me panting as I try to maintain control, pumping in and out of her until I have to force myself to stop to keep from blowing my load. My arm snakes between her breasts, tightening around her neck like a leash. Then, as I lean back to rest against my legs, she slides with me. I squeeze her neck, holding her in place, pumping into her. She arches her back against my chest as her pussy clenches around me repeatedly. Her orgasm crests as she cries out in ecstasy. It's music to my ears. My other hand reaches around to stroke her sensitive clit, sending her over the edge again. This time, while she throbs and clenches, she cums again, her hot liquid coating me. I slam into her faster, deeper, until my moans echo hers and I'm filling her full of my cum.

"So ruined and spent. Full of my cum." I rasp, reaching into the pocket of my sweats to retrieve the rag I soaked in brake fluid in order to knock someone out if I needed to tonight. I didn't except to use it on her, but then again, I didn't expect to fuck her either.

She doesn't say anything, still catching her breath as my dick pulsates inside of her.

"You took me so well, my little masterpiece. Thank you for being mine. I'm sorry." I slip the rag over her nose and mouth and wait for her to go limp.

When she does, I slide out to clean us both up. I keep the rag on her face so she steadily breathes in the fumes, keeping her unconscious while I erase every trace of our encounter here. Once I've finished, I scoop her into my arms and carry her home. I know exactly what I'm doing as I creep my way through the alley. Her boyfriend isn't home, so it's easy to slip inside the house undetected.

Inside, I work quickly to wash her down with a rag, cleansing her of our encounter together. I take extra care to make sure her body is clean. Even going so far as to wipe the wet rag across the folds of her pussy. After I finish washing her, I dress her in fresh pajamas and tuck her into bed. I place a trash can beside the bed on top of a towel. Grabbing a bottle of wine from the fridge in her bathroom, I pop it open and pour it down the drain, then stage the room. It's important for it to look like she had a normal night with maybe a little too much wine, which will explain the nausea and vomiting from the brake fluid.

Satisfied and certain I've covered my tracks, I slip out and away back to the body I left earlier so I can dispose of it, burning the evidence, every trace of it.

The shadows of night will be gone soon, and it's important the body is gone too. I haul it back to Amanda's house to burn it down to ash and spread all over the garden. It's better to make it disappear this way. The gang tags were only a temporary solution in case someone found it before I had time to circle back. She'll be asleep for the rest of the night, and I can watch over her from here as I hack up the body into smaller pieces on the tarp in her backyard.

Under the fading glow of the moon as I work to burn the last bits of him, I have an idea. It's a wonderfully wicked idea. I'm going to keep a little something as a souvenir. A little something I can send to Amanda later to remember this night. Tonight was better than I expected. I can't wait to fuck my masterpiece again, a perfect little play toy, built just for me and only me. I never want her to forget it.

BETRAYAL

Chapter Seven

Amanda

Sun slips past the barrier of the shutter blinds, warming my face with soft fall morning rays. Before I even open my eyes, I feel the waves of nausea threatening to spill the entire contents of my stomach. My head is pounding. It feels like shards of glass are digging into it. *Why do I feel like this? Am I sick?* I pry one eyelid open first, then the other. My bed is empty. Of course, he's either already gone to work or he slept in the spare bedroom, so I didn't wake up. I glance around the room. My book is tossed haphazardly on the bed, a wine glass is tipped over on my end table, and next to it is an empty bottle. Next to the bed is a trash can carefully placed on top of a towel. My clothes are halfway in the hamper and spilling out the front. I must have had a rough night. I remember I had to work late because the hospital was busy. We had three trauma calls come in right as the shift was ending and it was all hands on deck for almost two hours after that. Everything is a blur. I can't really remember anything else about last night.

I try to sit up but fall back, gripping the edge of my mattress. Tears roll down my cheeks. My head is throbbing. I can't remember the last time I had a headache this bad. A familiar salty taste fills my mouth, warning me I'm about to vomit. My stomach gives a lurch and I dive over the edge of the bed, hoping to make it into the trash can. When I've puked until I can't puke anymore, I squeeze my eyes shut and drift back to sleep.

I don't know how long I've slept for, only that the day is fully underway and sunshine is filling my room, bursting from every small crack it can make its way through. I'm terrified to sit up. *Maybe I can crawl to the bathroom for a glass of water.* I ease my way off the bed and onto my bedroom floor, dragging my body across the carpet to the cold dark bathroom in search of water, too afraid of what will happen if I try to lift my head more than a few inches.

Of course, once I'm sipping on small gulps of water in the bathroom, I realize my phone is still in bed. I'll have to crawl all the way back to where I left it, just to text him good morning. The cold tile floor feels so good against my burning skin. My stomach stops cramping and I finally feel the nausea ease up a bit. I twist the cap back on the water. My bed is so far away and not nearly as cold despite the cooling gel mattress. I close my eyes and rest my forehead against the cold flooring to silence the screaming headache. It helps enough that once again I drift off to sleep, only to wake feeling like I need to vomit a few minutes later. I barely make it over to the toilet. Having a hangover from hell is not my idea of a good time on my day off. *Why did I drink so much last night?* I wonder, *I can't remember anything after I got off work. Maybe we need to swear off drinking, Amanda.* My subconscious voice taunts, ridiculing me for my blackout drinking. I sigh. My headache flares, sending twinges of pain shooting through my brain, reminding me why I crawled instead of walked to the bathroom to begin with. Sitting up—even if it is just to throw up—is at least manageable now, which means at the very least I no longer have to crawl back to my bedroom. Ignoring the stabbing pain in my head, I pull myself up to standing and make my way back to bed to grab my phone.

I have a text message from my boyfriend waiting for me. It says he's sorry he snuck off early this morning for work and he hopes I've slept in because I was passed out when he got home last night and it looked like I drank an entire bottle of wine. I message him back quickly to tell him I'm awake and I have regrets, then allow my head to fall into the soft embrace of my pillow as I squeeze my eyes shut and try my best to remember last night. I retrace my night, memory by memory. This time I make it as far as getting on the light rail and riding home. Flashes and glimpses of the gym flash through my memory. I don't remember going to the gym last night and I don't see my gym clothes with the laundry when my eyes dart across the room. *This is so weird. Did I go to the gym last night or not?* I retrace my night from the beginning once more.

Bits and pieces are coming back to me more clearly now. I remember something happened, someone was following me and I ran. I was too afraid to run home and instead I ran to the gym. An image of the masked man pops into my head and I scream, my body trembling uncontrollably. I remember everything. There was no bottle of wine or reading. Last night, I hooked up with my masked stalker in the gym and I loved every minute of it. As the realization of what happened hits me, I hyperventilate. I'm having a full-blown panic attack and trying my best to calm down. This isn't the kind of thing I want to tell my boyfriend over a text. Instead, I send him a message to see how much longer until he can come home. There's no time for me to wait for a reply as I hit send the doorbell rings.

I jump from the bed in a panic. The doorbell. *Who could be here?* I check the camera. There's a package sitting on the front step, but it's just sitting there with no one around. I try to go back and see if the camera recorded the motion detection, but the motion detector never triggers. There's no video, only the live view of a package hanging out on my doorstep. Go figure this happens after I've completely freaked myself out and convinced myself that I willingly fucked a man in a mask in the gym to save my life. *You can't just leave a package sitting on the front porch, Amanda. Go bring it inside.* Something so simple and yet I'm terrified to leave the safety of my room. What if it's a trick like those articles you read online of women hearing crying and opening their front doors? A shiver runs down my side and

I zone out, silently arguing and hyping myself up enough to go retrieve the package.

I edge my way down the stairs with my back against the wall the entire time, my eyes sweeping the downstairs for someone else. It's impossible not to question my sanity right now. I mean, I woke to find myself in bed with one of my favorite stalker romance books, an empty bottle of wine and what feels like the worst hangover I've ever had. *Did I go to the gym and live out my fantasies with a masked stalker, or did I fall asleep reading one of my favorite books?* I don't have time to keep debating things with myself. I've reached the landing at the bottom of the stairs and the only thing standing between me and this very normal, very average-looking package is my front door. My hands shake as I twist the lock over. I poke my head out just enough to perform a quick scan of the neighborhood. The streets are empty. It's just me and the box. I take a deep breath then scramble out quickly, snatching it from the cement and scurrying back inside, twisting the lock closed behind me. Acting like a senseless lunatic, I turn to run back up the stairs, then stop, pivoting to run to the kitchen and open the package. Then I freeze, turning once more toward the stairs and take one step before pausing and making one definitive mad dash for the kitchen. I mindlessly disregard the rest of my surroundings in the house as I race to the kitchen, slam the box on the counter, and reach into the knife drawer to pull out something to cut it open.

The knife cuts through the tape easily, and the cardboard flaps bounce open. I lay the knife down on the countertop and bend the flaps open to reveal—

My body launches itself at the kitchen sink as my stomach heaves again. Tears run down my face as I wipe at them with the back of my hand and bolt upstairs, slamming the door shut behind me and locking it. Quivering, I mash the buttons on my phone. My boyfriend answers on the second ring.

I don't give him time to say anything. "Come home. I need you to come home right now. I'm not okay."

"Amanda, what's going on? I'm on my way. Stay on the phone with me. What's going on?"

I take a deep breath. "I'm sorry. I fucked up. I hooked up with a guy wearing a mask at the gym last night. He followed me there. I don't even know who he was, but," I stammer, trying to ground myself. "I'm so sorry. Part of me was so afraid. I watched him though, babe. Before the gym, I watched him stab some guy walking home from the light rail stop."

He laughs.

"Why are you laughing?" I shout.

"Amanda, I can't tell if you're being serious right now or you're trying to be funny and see how I will react." He says.

I open my mouth to respond, then stop myself. I must sound insane. "Just come home. I need you to see this for yourself. He was at the house."

"Who was at the house? You aren't making sense." He replies.

"The man. He was at the house. He rang the doorbell, and he left a box on the front step. Check the cameras. He left a box and when I brought it inside to open it up, there was a pair of eyeballs inside. Human eyeballs!" I scream frantically as more tears run down my face.

"Calm down. I'm on my way. The cameras go directly to my phone. I haven't had a notification all morning. I think you're having a bad day. You're hungover and clearly stressed out from yesterday. Go get in the shower and calm down. I'll be there soon. Have you eaten anything?" He asks.

"No, I haven't eaten. I've been throwing up all morning." I snap.

He sighs and I can sense his annoyance with my answer. He thinks I'm crazy and who can blame him? Shit, even I'm beginning to think I'm crazy.

"Get in the shower. I'm stepping into the elevator at the parking garage and I'm going to lose you. Don't worry, I'll be there as soon as I can. Call me back if you need to."

"Love you," I whisper before hanging up.

Do I though? I think. *Do I love him? He obviously doesn't believe me. But if I were him, would I believe me?* I look around my room. It looks like I came home after losing a trauma patient, downed a bottle, went to bed with a book, passed out, and woke up a train wreck. It doesn't look like I went to the gym, fucked a masked guy, almost died, watched someone get stabbed, and then found a pair of eyeballs sealed inside of a box on my doorstep. The eyeballs, though. That's my proof. Maybe I should bring them up here with me. I shudder at the thought. I don't want to even be in the same house as them. Thinking about it makes my stomach turn.

"He's right." I say to myself. "Go take a shower, Amanda."

I need to clear my mind and figure out exactly what happened last night. Everything feels overwhelming, like the world is crashing down around me as I walk into the bathroom and turn the shower on, setting the temperature to burning hot and letting it heat up before I step inside. Then I take the longest, hottest shower I've taken in a really long time. My entire body is feeling so much better and the effects of my hangover are finally wearing off. I've been in the shower for nearly half an hour, which means my boyfriend should be here any minute. I shut off the water and step onto the bath mat. When I do, the doorbell rings. My blood runs cold all over again and my heart races. What now? I check the live camera view, but there's no one there and there's no recording either. Maybe I really am losing my fucking mind.

COUNTDOWN

Chapter Eight

Amanda

My application for mental health-based leave from work was approved. It's taken me a few days to come to terms with stepping away to take care of myself, and I know my boyfriend is secretly hoping he can convince me not to go back ever. It's been five days since my psychotic breakdown. He hasn't left my side, except to work in his home office, since he came home and found me distraught. It's the first time he's left me home alone. I begged him for breakfast from the coffee shop and bakery down the street. I actually feel a little guilty about feeling smothered because he was so excited to get us a morning treat. When he left, I curled up in the living room chair to binge watch my favorite television series, which is all I've done for days. My therapist prescribed me some anti-anxiety medication, but I hate the way it makes me feel. I've been pretending to take them, because I'm not a fan of medication and the way it makes me feel disconnected from myself. I've treated way too many people for addiction in the emergency room. I've been hiding them under my tongue then spitting them into the toilet so he doesn't notice. Honestly, I'm not sure how my boyfriend would feel about a more natural approach—considering these are prescribed—but something tells me if it meant I would stay at home and let him provide for me, he'd give it a pass. I roll my eyes at myself and my internal monologuing.

I mentally run through the events of the last few days. When he arrived, I was in bed curled up around the pillows, dozing in and out of sleep, mentally exhausted. The second he woke me up, I took one look at him and completely broke down. He spent at least twenty minutes trying to get me calmed down and then when I led him downstairs to see the package of eyeballs on the kitchen counter, nothing was there. Even the knife I know I left on the countertop was back exactly where it belonged. He pulled up all the video footage. Nothing was there. There wasn't even a video of me opening the front door.

My boyfriend is the one who convinced me to take some mental health time and helped me complete all the paperwork. He even emailed it over to my boss for me and made sure my therapy appointments were all set up for virtual. He knows I'm too terrified to leave the house right now. I sigh. How is it that this man is so sweet? He takes the best care of me, goes above and beyond for me all the time, except in the bedroom. It's been over a month, almost two, since the last time we were intimate. I'm sure he hasn't tried anything recently because he's worried about me, but it's just so confusing. How can everything about him be absolutely perfect and here I am, ungrateful that our relationship isn't built on sex? *Maybe you're more messed up than you realize.* I chastise, turning my attention back to the TV and desperately try to unsuccessfully shut my brain off.

It doesn't matter. I'm off work until after Halloween. I have strict instructions to check in weekly with the therapist and take it easy. Plus, I'm not allowed to read any more stalker romances or books with lots of triggers until I'm feeling better. Everyone thinks I dreamed it all up. Even I'm beginning to realize they're probably right. Losing patients is always hard, but this last one messed me up more than I realized. I should be thankful to have such a supportive partner, instead of thinking about how much I wish he would just rail me.

I take a deep breath. Today begins my countdown to Halloween. I'm a member of the spooky-bitches-for-life club, and no amount of anxiety is going to rob me of an opportunity to celebrate the crap out of my favorite holiday this year. Besides, it will help me stay distracted, so long as I don't watch anything too terrifying. Scary movies move over, spooky season vacation from work begins to-day.

Part Two

Days Until Halloween

TEMPTATION

Chapter Nine

Mask

Night surrounds everything, cloaking me in its dark embrace. I've been watching her for hours. It's the first time we've been together since the other night. She hasn't gone to work in days. In fact, she hasn't left the house since our little soirée at the gym. I suppose I'm partially responsible for that. My mind trails off, remembering the time we spent together. I want to have her again. I need to have her again. It's all I've thought about for days. That's why I'm here. This withdrawal—the inability to see her like this—mixed with the thrill and excitement of it all, is unbearable. I had to see her. I had to visit my little masterpiece.

I miss so many things about her. The way she smells, the way her body moves when she walks, the sound of her voice. She's all tucked away, safe and sound, far away from me. It's not fair. There's nothing I can do but wait it out. She'll venture out again, and I'll be right here waiting for her when she does.

I've been working on a bit of a back-up plan for if she doesn't leave the house soon. A worst case scenario option. Halloween night is the perfect opportunity for me to slip into the house undetected, and take what I'm craving. She felt so good around me. Her cum left my cock smelling like her for hours. I'm craving her body again, and Halloween is still two weeks away. My hand knowingly slides into my sweatpants as I watch her from the patio chair in her back-yard. She's sleeping on the couch again. The rise and fall of her chest is steady as the TV blares in the background. She doesn't know that she's actually all alone. She thinks her boyfriend is just upstairs working, like he always says. The truth is, he's sneaking out and keeping secrets. For a brief moment, I consider slipping inside and touching her. My fingers ache to touch her supple skin, to feel it beneath their grip. I want to run them over her the way I did a few nights ago. Except I can't risk her waking up. Two weeks might be a long time, but it's the best chance I'll have at taking her again. The only chance I'll have to feel her tight, wet pussy coming all over my dick.

My grasp tightens and I imagine I'm thrusting into her instead of jerking off in her backyard while I watch her sleeping. I study the object of my obsession closely. Amanda Jenkins, twenty-five, and a nurse at the local community hospital. She has long, blonde hair that sparkles beneath the sunlight. It usually falls in waves around her face. But tonight she wears her hair pulled back in some kind of intricate braid. She's not wearing makeup—she doesn't need to. Her beauty is the rare beauty that radiates from within her. She's the kind of natural beauty every man dreams of. A goddamn masterpiece, just like the sunflowers swaying in the breeze along the back fence line. Every seed and every petal uniquely beautiful, just like her. I close my eyes and picture her face staring back at me in the mirror while I fucked her. My hand tugs on my cock harder and faster. I'm in more of a hurry than usual. Normally she's a creature of habit but, without work to dictate her day, she's become unpredictable. She could open her eyes right now and see me jerking off on her patio furniture from the window. I shrug my shoulders, thinking about it. So what if she did? It's not like she would do anything about it. She'd be far too afraid to call the police, and if she runs upstairs in search of her precious lover, she'll find he's not even home and nowhere to be found. My lips turn up into a sinister smirk. The entire time I've spent stalking her, I've been paranoid she'll catch me, and now I almost want her to wake up. I want to relish in the rush of adrenaline pumping through my veins.

I open my eyes to make sure she's not watching me back and secretly hoping she is. It's far too quiet. If she could see me jerking off, I'm pretty sure she would scream. My cock tightens, my excitement growing. I love the way she screams. Fuck. I'm close, so very close to coming as I watch the round curves of her breasts rising and falling while I pump faster. I think about how fucking hot it was to watch those pretty lips of hers surrounding my cock, suctioned around it as her tongue lapped over my sensitive nerves. My release is closing in as I replay the way she swallowed every inch of me. Even in my memories, I'm hypnotized, unable to stop myself from picturing her. Suddenly, it hits me. The familiar tug of relief is about to go pulsing through me. My cum shoots out in a steady stream; each stroke dropping more to the ground between my feet with a splatter. That's just what I needed, even if it doesn't compare to the way she felt when I was pounding her desperate little cunt.

Only two more weeks, I remind myself. I can make it two more weeks and then on Halloween night I'll finally get to take what's mine again. If I have to wait that long, it will be worth every minute. The anticipation alone is already driving me wild.

DREAD

Chapter Ten

Amanda

I must have dozed off on the couch earlier watching TV. The sun no longer fills the house with natural light. Instead, it splashes dark shadows across the room and up the walls. Above me it sounds like a door creaks open, except no one else is here. It's the first time I've been home alone since my incident. I thought it would feel good to have some space back after being smothered for a week, except now there's too much space. It's too empty, and I don't want to be alone. I take a deep breath. *Everything is okay. You're just freaking yourself out,* I think to myself. I desperately wish I could time travel to the end of the day, to the part where he comes home so we can curl up with one another and I can sleep against him while he works from his tablet. Consistency has been nice, having a structured schedule, even if it is a schedule full of nothing, has been peaceful. It doesn't always have to be a schedule full of nothing, though. I could find a purpose for my time. I also like working at the hospital and giving back to the community. Maybe I could cut back to part-time. He's not even here keeping me company, and he's in my head trying to convince me to just let him take care of me.

Groaning, I check the time again. It will be dark soon. The sun is dropping, painting shadows all over the house. My pumpkin spice-scented candle flickers on the coffee table, casting more shadows. It's my cue to flip on all the lights in the living room, entryway, and kitchen. As I flip on the light in the entryway, I swear I hear what sounds like footsteps in the room above me. I scurry to the kitchen to pull out a knife and listen. When ten minutes have passed, I decide to return to the living room. I pull a blanket out of the bin and cozy back up on the couch. My heart is hammering in my chest while my thoughts run away into a panicked frenzy of imaginary what if scenarios. All I'm doing is scaring myself more. The silence of the house must be getting to me. *Anxiety is so much fun—not,* I think with a sigh.

I turn on a not-scary Halloween movie and grab my phone for a little doom scrolling to distract me from my thoughts. I just need something else to think about for a little while until he comes home. Only one more hour, and in a little while I'll order us a pizza so I can surprise him with dinner and a movie. I'm sure his first day back at the office was grueling and even though I know he loves to cook for me, I don't want him to feel like he needs to.

There's a loud commotion outside. The garbage cans clang over, landing on the cement in the alley. I run to the window, snatching the blinds open enough to peer out of the gap I just created. It's only dusk, so there's still some light out. I wait patiently to see if anything or anyone emerges. It's not uncommon for stray animals to forage in the trash this time of year. It could be a cat or even my neighbor. I laugh nervously. I'm about to chalk it up to my imagination when a man-sized person in a black hoodie stands up, looks around the alley, then bolts off in the opposite direction. He looks back over his shoulder and I swear I spot the laces and the mask from the other night. My body shudders and I squint out the window, trying to catch another glimpse, but whoever it was is gone. I can't say for sure that I saw a mask, but it's definitely all

I can think about as I back away to check the locks on the back and front doors. I wrap the blanket around me protectively; the way a child might in order to feel safe while watching a scary movie, but it does little to comfort me or protect me from the terrors of the real world.

My phone buzzes. It's a text. He's on his way home. I stare at the message for a few minutes, trying to decide whether or not I should tell him about the alley or what I think I saw. After intense deliberation, I decide not to. It was his first day back; I don't want to worry him or make him feel any guiltier than I'm sure he already does. *Tonight is going to be a nice night,* I think as I rewind my movie to where I left off and order the pizza. He should be home before our dinner gets here, which means I won't have to worry about being too afraid to open the door for the delivery person. *Get a grip, Amanda.* I silently scold, frustrated by my amplified anxiety. *Day by day,* I apologize in an attempt to forgive myself.

While I wait for the pizza and my perfect gentleman of a boyfriend, I selfishly allow my thoughts to wander. *If he thinks today was just a normal day and I act like everything is okay, maybe, just maybe, he will be interested enough to have sex with me finally. It's been over a month, nearly two.*

I zone out waiting, completely engrossed in the movie from my childhood. It's nostalgic and checking all the boxes I've been in need of to feel better. Out of nowhere, a pair of hands land over my eyes and soft lips brush against my jaw.

"Surprise," his voice rumbles.

It's not until my brain processes everything that my heart stops racing. I know that voice and I know those lips. Even his smell is familiar.

He wraps me in a hug over the back of the couch. "Did you notice if an animal got into the trash cans today? They were all toppled over in the alley. I picked the mess up. There were several ripped open bags."

I shrug. Part of me wants to tell him I thought I saw the masked man from before, and part of me wonders if

I should take the medication I was prescribed. My mind is racing full of what ifs and possible reactions to both.

"Baby," he prompts. "Did you hear me?"

"Oh sorry," I lie, too easily. "I keep getting really sucked into this movie."

"I was just asking if you saw anything or heard anything with the trash cans today. It looks like something got into them." He says.

I decide to just be honest. "I know you won't believe me, but I'm pretty sure I saw him again."

"Saw who again?"

"The man in the mask I told you about." I reply.

"Damnit, Amanda. We've been over this. There wasn't a man in a mask. Have you been taking your medication? Was today too much for you? I can work from home if I need to, luxuries of being the boss." His tone is laced with concern as his eyes sweep over me.

"It's fine. You're right. It's probably just my eyes playing tricks on me. You said it looked like animals got into it. The wind probably knocked them over, and a raccoon or something got into them." I rattle off.

It's not worth trying to convince him of anything. No one believes me. I don't even know if I believe me.

"Do you mean that, Amanda?" He asks.

"Yes." Another lie.

What I really think is that the masked man knocked things down, and an animal got into it afterward, but there's no sense pleading with him to believe me.

"How about I stay home tomorrow?" He offers.

"No." I respond a little too quickly.

"No?" He sounds hurt.

Fuck, this is exactly why you shouldn't lie. It's a slippery fucking slope. The lies are just sliding off my tongue tonight. "No, because Erica and I are planning a coffee date in the next few days and I need some self-care to pull myself together. I don't need you to stay home with me. I want things to go back to normal. No, I need things to go back to normal." *Well, at least part of that ended up being the truth.*

"If you're sure. But, Amanda, it's not an inconvenience. If you want me to stay with you—if you change your mind—all you have to do is ask."

He's so fucking sweet and charming, while I sit here lying to his face. I feel like such an asshole. I don't have long enough to dwell on it. The doorbell rings and I welcome the escape.

"I think that's dinner. Do you mind getting the door?"

He doesn't say anything but he walks off, a bit defeated, to answer the door. I pause the movie and click back to the Home Screen to pull up his favorite. So what if I'm feeling guilty? I need to get out of this house. A coffee and shopping date sound equal parts amazing and terrifying.

CRAVING

Chapter Eleven

Mask

It's exactly one week from Halloween. I expected her to leave the house by now, but she hasn't. She appears to be perfectly content, locked away inside the house day after day. She even started doing yoga in the living room yesterday. Meanwhile, my nightly sessions spent jerking off while watching her through the windows of the house have become less exciting. It's not as fun to imagine now that I've had an authentic experience. It's the closest thing I have to fucking her though and I've endured far worse forms of torture. In my surveillance room, the six different monitors flash views of her house. I almost got busted installing these yesterday when she woke up from her nap and I'm almost certain she glimpsed me in the alley.

My withdrawals are getting the best of me. I had to do something, and it meant getting creative. If I can't stalk my little masterpiece home from work every day, then how else am I supposed to see her? It's not like I could continue showing up outside her house in broad daylight. It would look oddly suspicious. I don't need to attract any unwanted attention, so I've simply slipped in a few times during her afternoon naps. It's given me all the opportunity I need to wander around without having to worry about getting caught, and plenty of time to install a few cameras.

She's going to be all alone tonight for a few hours and because she's a sexually-depraved creature of habit, I know exactly how she intends to use the time. I lean back in my nice plush gaming chair, eye the door to make sure it's locked, pop my headphones on, and click around until I have her on the screen. I watch intently as she makes her way upstairs. First checking the lock on the front door, then she tiptoes up the stairs slowly. At the top, she veers off to the bedroom. I watch her on the screens as she wanders around her room collecting supplies for a bath. She makes multiple trips into the bathroom and starts the water. While she waits for the tub to fill, she heads to her nightstand and pulls out a few toys.

Jackpot. Grabbing my belt and ripping it off my pants in a flash, I unbutton my pants then pull my cock out, gripping it firmly. I can't wait for my favorite show to begin. There's nothing else I enjoy watching more than this right here. Well, actually now that I think about it, there is one thing I would love to watch again. I haven't been able to stop replaying what it was like watching me fuck her in the mirror at the gym. A low moan escapes my lips as I slide my hand up my shaft slowly. Taking extra care not to be too rough around the barbell, remembering how much she enjoyed running her tongue across it when I was fucking her pretty mouth. I watch my girl undress. She's like a sunflower—a masterpiece of nature, and every glance I steal feels like temptation. I fight the urge to go to her knowing she longs to be touched, to experience the satisfaction a man can provide and I am more than eager to satiate her hunger.

I stroke myself harder, more aggressively, watching as she sinks into the bubbles filling the tub full of hot water. Candles flicker, casting shadows that dance across the screen. She pops her earbuds in. What a naughty girl she is, listening to an audiobook. I wish I knew which one so I could listen along with her. I'll have to settle for the sound of her sweet moans. She doesn't even realize she's making them with her earbuds tucked in her ears and the audiobook playing. It's so fucking addicting the way she turns me on. My cock twitches in agreement, pre-cum leaking out and over my fingers. I rub it over myself, imagining it's her cum all over me like the last time we were together. The smell of her on my dick the next morning was almost more than I could handle. I want to taste her cum in my mouth. Groaning, I think about plunging two fingers into her tight, wet pussy, then pulling each one out to lick them clean.

As if she can read my mind, her hand dips beneath the bubbles and presumably between her legs to stroke her needy little cunt. I want to fill it for her, stretching her all around me until she has every inch of me inside of her, throbbing as she clenches her warm walls against me—Fuck!

If I don't slow down, I'm going to cum before the good part. I take a deep breath and focus on waiting for my stunning goddess to catch up. It's true, I could watch her for hours. A chuckle rolls off my lips. I *do* watch her for hours. It's my obsession. I can watch her anywhere, anytime. Every inch of her is crafted to pull me closer, every flaw only making her more real, more mine.

Amanda's hand surfaces and reaches for her favorite toy as I begin to drag my hand over my cock slowly. My eyes close, imagining her running the vibrating silicone all over her pussy, teasing her clit until small cries escape her lips and she drops her head back to rest against the cool tile, panting as she works herself over. I watch her on my screen as she cums, pumping myself faster until my cum explodes out and onto my stomach. I groan, filled with a deep satisfaction, but it's only a temporary fix. All I can think about is fucking her again. *Soon,* I think. *It's almost Halloween. Only a few more days until I'm fucking her again.*

FACADE

Chapter Twelve

Amanda

We did not have sex, which I expected, and the bed was empty when I woke up. Erica is coming to pick me up for a pumpkin spice-themed morning at the coffeehouse. Otherwise, I'd spend the afternoon like I always do: watching Halloween movies and napping on the couch while I wait for my boyfriend to get home from work. This is my first adventure out since I started my mental health leave. I need to get it over with though so I can try to get back into my routine since I'll be returning to work in a few weeks.

I kick the blankets back and stare out the window at the bleak and stormy day. The weather is perfect for fall. There's a light drizzle falling from the sky. The tiny raindrops stick to my window, greeting me for the day. It's as if Mother Nature knew I needed a day like today. Rainy days are my favorite. This also means it will be cold enough for an oversized Halloween sweater. I swing my feet out of bed and trudge off to the bathroom to get ready for our breakfast date. Once I've tidied my hair and put on a light layer of makeup, I head to my closet to dress, selecting a comfortable pair of fleece-lined fake leather yoga tights and my frayed, army green sweater with black pumpkins.

My phone chimes as I am scrutinizing my outfit in the mirror. I swipe it open to read that text from Erica, letting me know she's on her way to pick me up. Before I can text her back, there's a knock on the front door. I freeze, my heart thunders in my ears and the panic creeps over me. *Not today,* I think to myself. *I just want to feel normal. The thought of having to answer the front door absolutely terrifies me, but it shouldn't.* I try to give myself a pep talk, working up enough courage to at least make my way to the upstairs landing. I glance down at my phone, remembering the front door camera, and check the app. It's strange it doesn't even show the front door camera has been activated. The app shows the camera is off instead and flashing low battery. That's inconvenient. I silently battle myself in my head, trying to decide whether or not I am brave enough to go to the door. I take a deep breath and descend the stairs slowly, one step at a time. When I reach the bottom, I carefully tiptoe across the entryway to the large window next to the front door to peek out around the edges of the curtain to see if anyone is there. The curtains are thick and heavy to keep the heat out in the summer and in during the winter. It makes them easier to pull a small fold aside. When I gaze out, my eyes search the porch. It's empty except for a bouquet of black sunflowers. My favorite flowers. It's why we have so many along the back fence line near the garden. I ordered black sunflower seeds from the internet, and gleefully planted them. When they finally grew, there were no black sunflowers in the bunch. I laugh to myself, remembering how disappointed I was. My boyfriend searched all over the city and came home the next day to surprise me with some he found at a local florist. *Maybe these are from him,* I think, twisting the deadbolt over slowly and easing the door open just enough to dash out quickly and swipe the flowers from the step.

There's a card rubber-banded to them, but I don't read it until I'm back inside the safety of the house with the heavy wood door locked again. I take the flowers to the kitchen and lay them on the counter. My hands tremble as I slide open the card to reveal a handwritten note. "Masterpiece," is all it reads. It's not signed, but there's only one person they could be from, right? Except I distinctly remember the masked man calling me a masterpiece, but that was a dream, so I can't remember it. Shaking, I fall to the ground, pulling my knees into my body, still clutching the card between my fingers. Hot tears fill my eyes, threatening to spill over the brims and ruin my makeup. I drop the card on the ground without a thought and stand up to grab a paper towel from the countertop. Eyeing the flowers wearily as I dab and blot the tears away before they can run down my face, smearing my makeup. I don't want Erica to know about this.

Go figure, my phone buzzes and I know it's her letting me know she's here. A car horn honks and that's all the confirmation I need to know it's Erica without even having to check my text. I don't have time to think about the flowers anymore, and honestly I don't want to. I just want to go have a nice normal breakfast with my friend, then come home and have a nice normal afternoon spent on the couch watching a Halloween movie. *Normal. Is that so much to ask for, universe?*

I set the house alarm and lock the door, then toss the keys in my bag, planting a big fake smile on my face so she doesn't think anything is wrong.

"Girl, look at you all cute and Halloweened up for our little coffee date," Erica hollers at me from the car.

My fake smile transforms into a genuine one, and I wave at her. She always has the best compliments. My life would be incredibly dull without my partner in crime, even though we don't see each other nearly as much as we should. I open the car door and slide inside. She has the seat warmer pre-heated for me, making the leather nice and cozy. I snuggle in, relaxing, and click my seatbelt into place.

"I should let you dress me from now on. You look hot today, like you just stepped out of a fall magazine," Erica pats my sweater. "It's soft, too. I'm so jealous."

I roll my eyes at her, and give her a once over. "You must be kidding me. Your accessory game is on point. The only reason you want me to dress you is because you know I ordered this from one of those boujee boutique websites on social media and you wish you grabbed a bunch for yours."

"Busted, and guilty. You know I can't help myself. Won't you please consider doing some stylist work on the side for me? You can curate an entire line all your own," she begs.

I laugh. "Oh yeah, and what would we call it? Lonely mood reader?"

But I think about her offer. That's something I could do if I actually quit my job. I could curate an adorable clothing line, market the crap out of it, and have a blast attending the giant clothing conventions she's always telling me about in Texas.

"He's still working late and never around, I take it?" Erica asks, her lips pursing together in a hard frown. She's been my ride or die since we moved into the dorms together freshman year. We instantly just clicked and ever since then, we've always been a little overprotective of one another.

"Yeah," I sigh as we pull into the coffee shop a few blocks away. One perk of living on the edge of the city is all the adorable shops and bistros sprinkled nearby. Erica's boutique is across the street from our favorite spot. It works out perfectly to meet for breakfast a few times a month. It's also near the gym and only a few shops away on the same street in the same shopping center. I glare at the gym, then quickly look away, hoping she didn't notice and was too busy focusing on parallel parking.

She sandwiches the car into the spot, perfectly shifting into park and cutting the engine.

The door jingles when we walk inside. The aroma of freshly ground coffee and sweet pastries hits my nose instantly. My stomach rumbles and I realize I am a lot hungrier than I thought. We don't bother stopping at the counter. Justin will swing by with all of our favorite seasonal treats. We booked ahead with him last week to reserve all our favorites. He owns the coffee shop—and if you ask me, I think he has a bit of a thing for Erica, but she refuses to acknowledge it. I secretly think she likes him back, but they are both too stubborn and shy when it comes to the other to do anything about it. Erica waves at him behind the counter as we pass by on our way to our spot. I smile, knowing it's the little things like that wave that make me suspicious.

Our favorite table is small and nuzzled in the corner against the edge of one window with a view of the Main Street and many of the shops. It's perfect for people watching, which we love to do. We always have the best time making up strange backstories for our unsuspecting muses.

Once we've had a few minutes to get settled in, Justin smiles over at us and gives Erica a big wave back. He's cute. The two of them are perfect for one another. I've practically written them an entire meet-cute in my head, and neither one of them knows about it. It's probably better that way.

He pops over cheerfully a few minutes later with a tray full of fall goodies and our coffee orders.

"There's my two favorite locals," he says with a smile as he unloads everything onto the table skillfully from the gleaming silver serving platter.

Erica and Justin exchange witty banter for a few minutes, until he excuses himself. The coffee shop is always busy, he never has time to chat for long.

"He's cute," I blurt out bluntly, once he's out of earshot.

Erica blushes slightly. "And?" She replies.

"And the two of you would be cute together," I tease. "You should ask him out on a date. You know he would never have the confidence to ask you."

She laughs me off. "He's way out of my league. I could never."

"Babe, you're going to leave me no choice. If you won't, I'm definitely leaving your number scribbled on one of these napkins." I gesture to the pile of napkins on the table.

She quips an eyebrow at me. "Do what you must."

"You want me to leave your number on a napkin?" I ask, surprised at how little she is putting up a fight.

She shrugs. "Why not? What do I have to lose? If you make things weird, I guess we just have to find a new coffee shop. Or I tell him you finally broke up with your boyfriend, meant to write your number, then wrote mine by mistake in your mass hysteria and heartbreak."

It's my turn to look down my nose at her. "Bitch," I mumble before snatching a pastry from the arrangement in front of us.

"Proud of it," Erica says with a laugh.

We spend at least an hour eating and people watching before she invites me to see the store and some of the new things she just got in for the winter inventory. I scribble her number on a napkin as promised and we each leave a ten for a tip. I personally adore Justin and appreciate how hard he works to be the life of the coffee shop. It's a staple in our community. As we head out, we both wave goodbye to him.

"See you in a few weeks, ladies," he hollers at us.

DEVOTION

Chapter Thirteen

Mask

Amanda closes the door and locks it. I watch her hidden behind the neighbor's bushes. The frayed hem on her sweater sways across the small of her back as she skips down the front steps and climbs into the car. She's so fucking sexy in those tight, fake leather leggings. The way they cling to her body captivates my senses. I wish I could watch her walking home in those; or better yet, peel them off of her and slide my cock into that warm, tight pussy. My thoughts have me contemplating surprising her today. But Halloween is only three days away, and I have the perfect night planned for the two of us. As excited as I am to see her finally leaving the house, I make the difficult decision to go ahead with what I have planned instead of changing course. I've spent too much time coming up with an elaborate evening of fun. There's no sense in scrapping it for an impulsive romp. Waiting will only intensify how good it will feel to take her again. The house will be all mine for at least an hour, and if I finish with time to spare, I can make sure to walk my sweet little victim home.

Underneath my breath, I snicker. I really am a considerate stalker. Once the car is out of sight, I crawl out from my hiding spot and make my way around to the back of the house. Working quickly so as not to attract the looks of nosy neighbors, I lift the cover off the window well and jump down to the bottom. This is the perfect entry point. I've been searching for a good way in on Halloween; somewhere with no cameras. There's an alarm on the window but it's not blinking, indicating the batteries ran out ages ago. Someone really should be more on top of checking the security system. It's a shame the batteries in the doorbell just so happened to go out today, too. I stifle another snicker, although since the house is empty, there's no reason not to let it out.

The window slides open easily, just like I knew it would. I hop into the basement, landing with a thud on the cement, and unload the last camera I want to place in the house from my backpack, then look around for some-where to tuck it away until Halloween night. There's a crawl space at the back of the basement. I'm sure no one will dig around in there anytime soon. The backpack fits just inside the door and to the left perfectly. No one will know it's here but me. It has everything I need for Hal-loween stashed inside. I want to catch up with Amanda so I can keep an eye on her this morning. It's her first day out, and I need to ensure my little masterpiece is safe from everyone but me.

I don't waste any more time in the basement. My feet take the stairs two at a time to the main floor. I pop out of the basement door and hang a left down the hall to the kitchen. When I walk by, I notice the flowers carelessly tossed on the counter. What can I say? I'm a hopeless romantic. I can't just leave these exotic beauties to dry up and die. Waltzing into the kitchen, I poke around to find a vase, arranging the rare black sunflowers. The card from me is on the ground. I pick it up off the floor and place it on the countertop next to the vase full of sunflowers, gazing at them for a moment as my head fills with thoughts of Amanda. Her body is as fucking irresistible as breathing;

I need it so I can feel alive. Every nerve in my body pulses with desire for her touch.

I have to stop myself from thinking about her. The plan is to be in and out. I glance at the time on my watch. I better wrap this up so I can meet my obsession for coffee. She won't even realize I'm there. Satisfied with my work in the kitchen, I make my way through the rest of the house, stopping to place my camera in the family room. It's the one spot I haven't been able to hide one because I am too afraid of waking her up during her nap. The camera takes me less than fifteen minutes to set up and install. I'm back on schedule for our little rendezvous, and I can't wait to see her in those tight pants again.

When I am finished, I walk up the stairs to her bedroom. I originally intended to keep her panties the other night, but somehow I ended up leaving without them. *Any pair will do really*, I think to myself as I slide open her panty drawer to rifle through it. Once I find a pair I like, I tuck them in my pocket to take with me. Another quick glance at my watch tells me I've been here longer than I wanted. I leave her panties amiss, hoping she'll piece it together that I was here. Or maybe I'll simply just tell her I was and enjoy her reaction. Just because I'm not planning to fuck

Amanda today doesn't mean I can't play with my toy. I smile to myself, thinking about making a promise not to be gentle as I retrace my way back through the house, down into the basement, and out through the window, popping off the window sensor completely. Then I climb out and replace the cover. I don't want to take any chances of things going wrong on Halloween.

I check my watch again. Good, I might still have time to catch Amanda at the coffee shop. She's lucky to have me watching over her today. My lips curl up into a wicked grin as I run my hand through my hair, combing it out of my face. The wind is blowing the strands every which way and it's drizzling. I pull the hood on my sweatshirt over my head.

When I make it to the coffee shop, I'm ready for a nice warm cup. The temperature dropped faster than I thought it would. *Lucky me,* I think as I duck inside the door. The scent hits me first, flooding my nostrils with the tantalizing smell of fresh coffee mixed with sweet pastries. I scan the cafe in search of her. Thirteen. It took me thirteen seconds to find her. She's in one of her favorite spots. There's a table at the back of the store tucked far enough away that will allow me to watch her without being noticed. I slink off to it, pulling my hood around my head more, before sliding into the cool leather seat, so I can watch Amanda carefully. After I am settled, I scan the menu and order. I type in the number on my table and wait patiently for the barista girl to deliver my coffee order. It arrives promptly.

All the while I sip my coffee watching her. I watch everything about her. The way her lips tug and pull into a smile, and how her mouth fills with laughter before erupting with joy. Amanda is a stunning specimen. I could stare at her for hours and never tire of it. Too bad it appears she has other plans. She stands to leave and I wait patiently to see where they are going before I slink off after my sweet obsession. My masterpiece.

UNSETTLED

Chapter Fourteen

Amanda

Erica twists my arm, convincing me to ride over to the store with her so she can show off some of the new inventory. It's not like I have any big plans today besides my nap. It doesn't take much coercing on her part. Soon we are in the back room laughing and giggling as I continue to add odds and ends to my pile of clothes to try on.

"You know, I really could use the help with curating different lines. It wouldn't be much, but it would give you something to work with and the more you put into it, the more you'll get out of it." Erica casually suggests, as I hold up a black satin shirt.

"I'll think about it. Like actually though, I've been thinking a lot about quitting my job." I confess.

She gives me a questioning look. "Is this because he made partner?"

I nod. "He's like a really big boss now. It's been kind of nice having a little extra time to spend together since we usually have none. It's not much, but I'll take it."

Erica smiles. "Well, you seem really happy. I say do it. You only live once."

My face lights up with happiness. I can't believe I'm actually considering quitting, or at the very least dropping to part time. "Thanks, I need the encouragement. It feels uncomfortable to just rely on a man to take care of me. I've never had that before, and part of me would feel guilty."

"Don't feel guilty, Amanda. You got yourself a good one, even if he works a lot. He cares about you. You know I believe in you and I'll support any decision you make. I'm not just saying that because I want you to be my partner in crime."

"I know. That's why you are such a good friend." I give Erica a big hug.

She's given me a lot to think about. I have options, I'm loved, and all these doubts about my man are probably just nerves. Women everywhere would kill for a man who wants to take care of them and provide everything they need. I have to stop convincing myself he doesn't want me, or that something is wrong. I should appreciate that our relationship is built on so much more than intimacy.

I help Erica with her inventory and have a blast dressing up the mannequin. We spend some much needed time catching up. It's late afternoon by the time we finish. Erica has a meeting with the city council in an hour since she sits on the shopping center chamber of commerce. She offered to take me home, but I opted to walk. The last thing I want to do is inconvenience her by sending Erica the opposite direction and making her backtrack to the meeting. Besides, there's plenty of daylight and it won't be dark for a few hours.

She hesitates at first. "Are you sure? I can drive you."

"It's only a few blocks home," I quickly reassure her, gathering the clothes I picked out, pay her for them at an insanely steep discount because she insists, then wave goodbye.

"I promise I'll text you when I get home so you aren't worrying about me." I say, before turning to walk away.

I begin my trek home. It's two blocks back to the house and late afternoon. There's plenty of traffic around and oodles of sunlight. I convince myself I'm not worried, but deep down inside, I am riddled with anxiety. *Honestly, Amanda, you should have just asked Erica for a ride back home. She wouldn't have thought it was an inconvenience,* I scold myself as I cross the street.

I notice a man sitting alone outside the smoothie shop. His back is to me, so I can't see his face. He's wearing a black hoodie and sweatpants. I'm not sure why, but he makes me feel uncomfortable. I walk a little faster and soon I'm rounding the corner of the first block.

When I turn, my eye catches movement out of the corner and I spin around to nothing. There's no one there, but it feels like someone is following me. I have a nagging feeling in my gut, telling me I'm not alone. I cast a glance over my shoulder and immediately do a double take. For a minute I freeze, staring down the street. I'm certain a man in a black hoodie just dove down an alley and out of sight. It's not cold, but I shiver anyway.

Deep in my chest, my heart is pounding. I'm walking as fast as I can but still a half block from the corner that will lead me home. My blood is pumping so hard it whooshes in my ears. I chance another look back over my shoulder. I don't see anything, but when I turn back around, I run right into a large, firm, muscular body. Big strong hands envelope my waist, drawing me in close against his body so he can rasp into my ear.

"Hello, Masterpiece."

Fuck! My pussy shouldn't ignite at the sound of his voice, but it betrays me, erupting with burning, fervent desire. I knew I didn't imagine this. It was all far too real to have been a dream or figment of my imagination.

"I knew you were real," I whisper foolishly, not intending to say it out loud.

"Of course I'm real. If I wasn't real, would I be able to do this?" He asks, placing his hand between my thighs and forcing his fingers against me to rub over my pussy. It's wet and waiting for him.

Even it remembers how good he felt—and that piercing. Thinking about the way it felt to slide across it has me quickly turning into a puddly mess. He grinds his hand against me, more firmly this time, and a soft moan escapes my parted lips. My head falls back and the sunlight glistens in my eyes, blinding me long enough to snap back to reality. Still hazy with desire, I try to push away from him, but he stops me.

"Oh, tsk, tsk tsk, Amanda. What's the hurry? Be a good host and entertain me." His words drip with a lust filled danger coated venom as he grabs my hand and rubs it up and down his hard length.

When I don't willfully stroke him, he reaches into his pocket and pulls out the knife from the other night. "I said, be a good little whore and greet me properly, Masterpiece."

My nipples harden from the silky, alluring way his words set off alarms in my body. *You're sick, Amanda. You shouldn't be enjoying this.* But I am. In fact, I'm enjoying every bit of it. Even though I know I should run, I want to fuck him again. It's not fair, my life is perfect. Why does this masked man have to make everything so confusing? *Knee him right in the cock and run, Amanda.* My brain screams at me, but my feet remain firmly planted on the sidewalk.

Somewhere nearby a trash can crashes to the ground with a thud. He releases me, instantly caught off-guard. There are no second thoughts. This time my brain powers on my feet and I bolt, running as fast as I can back to the house.

"Run, run, run, little masterpiece. You can't hide from me. I know exactly where to find you," he bellows in his deep, raspy voice.

I look back over my shoulder, but he's gone, and I can't hear any shoes slapping against the concrete but my own. By the time I turn the corner, I'm panting hard, gasping for breath. I might be on the verge of an asthma attack, but I'm not stopping until I make it inside safely. My feet carry me racing up the front steps swiftly, where I stop to fumble with the door.

The moment it clicks open, I dive inside; terrified but safe. I'm not fucking crazy. This guy is real, and he's stalking me. I don't know how to feel or react. My body gives out and I slide to the ground, pulling my knees in and hugging them tightly. I sob, wrapping my arms around myself. *Why the fuck did I let any of that happen? What's wrong with me?* My body didn't just want him, it craved him. My pussy salivated for him. Even now, it throbs and aches at the thought of him. The memories from the other night came flooding back rapidly. The dangerous allure of his presence was enough to send every nerve in my body into an electric frenzy.

When I've calmed down and worked up enough courage, I peek through the slats in the blinds by the entryway, but just as I expected, the street is empty. It feels like I am losing my mind. I should have just had Erica drive me home. Fuck. Erica. I need to text her. I pull my phone out and shoot off a text, then immediately send off another text to my boyfriend asking if he's on his way home yet. He doesn't answer, but I figured he wouldn't.

What was I thinking, planning a day at home alone? I've been a mess lately, and now I'm texting him like a completely idiotic baby. It's no wonder he doesn't want to fuck me. It's no wonder my skin desperately begs for the feel of a masked psychopath's touch; unrelenting, starved, and claiming me for himself. I'm such a complete train wreck. How am I supposed to go back to work when I can't get a handle on my own psychotic episodes? Or maybe I just need to get a handle on my stalker. *Fuck. I really need to pull myself together,* I think as I allow myself to fall against the wall becoming one with it and the floor once more before stealing a look out the bottom of the window again, just to be sure he's not outside. There's nothing but a few lone leaves blowing down the street. *Get a grip, Amanda.*

I wait a few more minutes to see if I get a text back. When I don't, I pick myself up off of the floor and climb the stairs to my room. Water therapy and a good cry in the shower are exactly what I need right now. I have all the best intentions to get in the shower, but I stop short and fall into my bed. I grab one of my favorite comfort reads and curl up with a book. Damn, I've missed the escape reading brings me.

I don't even know how long I've been reading for when my boyfriend finally texts me back, but it's dark now, and I can tell from his one-word answer, *no,* that it won't be worth waiting for him. Despite wanting to ignore the rumble in my stomach, I decide I may as well make myself some dinner and, after the day I've had, a glass of wine to settle my nerves is perfectly reasonable. When I pass by the front door, I check to make sure both locks are set. In the kitchen, I grab a plate and build myself a mini charcuterie with cheese, meat, fresh fruit, and a handful of nuts. I pour myself a nice tall glass of wine, cork the bottle, and return it to the wine fridge. The wind blows the nearly bare tree branches against the kitchen window, making me jump.

It's okay, Amanda. It's only the wind. I reassure myself on my way back to the bedroom and my book. I pause at the bottom of the stairs, setting my wine on the entry table to tap the security screen and arm the house before heading upstairs.

In my room, I set my glass on a coaster from my last book box, and my plate next to it. Then I pull down the covers and toss my stuff onto the blankets. Before I climb into bed and get comfortable, I snatch the remote off his side and flip on another Halloween movie for some background noise. Satisfied, I slide into bed and snuggle in. I leave the curtain pulled open, intent on catching anyone who might be hiding in the shadows. I open the security app on my phone and make sure I have the notifications on.

"Cheers," I say, toasting my screen and switching to my e-reader, so I can use the stand and the remote to continue reading while I snack.

I settle back into my book, getting so immersed I completely lose myself within the pages. Things are getting spicy by the time I've drained my second glass and finished my snacks. It's time for an intermission and thirds, also known as finishing the bottle. I cast a side-eye at my bedside table and then the clock. Do I dare let myself get carried away, or is it cutting it too close to the time he has been getting home? I shrug, springing off the bed at the realization that maybe he will walk in on me and so what? Maybe it will take him from a vanilla boy to the men in my books. Just thinking about him getting into it and the way I imagine he might react has me hot. I snatch my phone, then race downstairs to pour the rest of the bottle into my glass in a hurry. His loss. This book is my favorite for a reason, and it's far too good to let a wasted opportunity pass by. From the bedside table drawer, I pull out my favorite toy. My fingers wrap around it in a familiar embrace. Tapping the screen, I dive back in. It's not long before I'm another half a glass deep. The soft buzz fills the room and I flip through page after page. All the while, my orgasm builds.

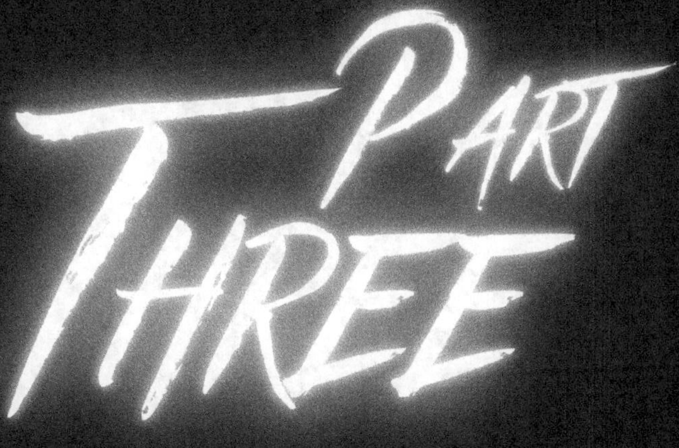

HALLOWEEN
NIGHT

7:30 AM

Chapter Fifteen

Amanda

It's Halloween. One of my favorite days of the year, or maybe it's the celebration of fall leading up to it. Halloween is like one last big shebang before snowflakes blow through the air and Jack Frost paints the world for winter. I blink my eyes open slowly, still unsure if I'm ready to greet the day yet. It's bittersweet really. The days are dwindling away as my time on leave runs out and my boyfriend's offer remains unclaimed. I have to decide soon. *There's Erica's offer too—and part time.* My brain is chiming off, running down an entire list of possibilities, and my day is only just beginning.

Ugh, I scoff at myself. Why am I like this? I rub my eyes and focus on clearing my mind, then open them again for a reset. This time, I notice purple and orange sticky notes everywhere. My hands fly up to my mouth in surprise as a million-dollar smile slides across my lips. This is seriously cute. A giddy squeal escapes my mouth as I leap to my feet and bolt across the room to collect a sticky note and read it. *Good morning, beautiful.* I look around the room for another one. I spot one on the TV that reads: *Halloween date night in? Say yes!* I can't stop smiling.

"Yes," I whisper to myself.

There's another note on the wall by the bathroom. *Happy Halloween!* On the mirror I find another note. *Have a boo-rific day.* Once I've washed my face and put a face mask on, I head downstairs for coffee. It's a misty, drizzly morning outside and it calls for my favorite Halloween mug. On the banister is a bright orange sticky note. *Find the boo basket.* Wow! I can't believe he made me a boo basket. At the bottom of the stairs, a purple sticky note waits for me innocently on the floor. *Check your email. I sent you book money.* I place this note in the pile I'm holding and continue into the kitchen. On the fridge there's another note waiting. *Breakfast will be delivered at eight.* I check the time. It's almost eight. Ten more minutes. I continue my scavenger hunt, wandering into the family room and spot a sticky note on the couch. *Quit your job. I had to try.* I toss my head back and laugh. He's persistent. My eyes sweep over the room in search of more notes or a boo basket. Eventually, I spot it nestled next to the fireplace, all cozy and perfect for fall. I skip over excitedly, only to find one last note. *I love you forevers and evers.*

I bite my thumb, feeling my eyes fill with burning hot tears, but I fight them back. The basket has some calming tea and all kinds of Halloween themed snacks and treats. There's a spooky-themed white fluffy blanket with black bats on it, and a pumpkin bath bomb. There are so many amazing things in the basket. I can't believe he made this for me. I send him a quick *thank you* text.

A knock on the door interrupts my thoughts. I panic for a moment and then remember it's breakfast. I check the doorbell camera to be sure, then realize how ridiculous this all is. After accepting the breakfast from the delivery woman, I breathe a sigh of relief. Answering the door shouldn't be scary, but it absolutely is. I have all day to prepare for date night and I want everything to be absolutely wonderful. Once I've finished my breakfast, I unpack the rest of the boo basket, setting up the holiday-themed snacks and treats in the kitchen. Then I prepare the candy bowl for trick-or-treaters tonight. I love trick-or-treaters, but we agreed with how unsettled I've been. It's probably better if I sit trick-or-treat out this year. At first I was disappointed, but deep down I knew my boyfriend was right. It's sweet of him to go through all this trouble to make up for missing out on some of my favorite Halloween things, like passing out candy and enjoying all the kids' costumes. Besides, there will be plenty more Halloweens in the years to come. Missing out on this one won't be that bad.

I spend most of the morning making sure everything is perfect for our date night in. My stomach gives a grumble reminding me I need to take a break and get something to eat. Coincidentally, the doorbell rings again. I'm not expecting any packages or anyone. Hesitantly, I check the camera but there's nothing showing up. No one is there, and it didn't even capture anything ringing it. *That's weird,* but I decide to check the porch for a package anyway. What with all the other surprises I woke up to, I can't just ignore it. And considering we have porch pirates all over the city, I don't want to chance leaving anything out there.

You can do this, Amanda. It's just like when breakfast arrived, giving myself a pep talk as I walk to the front door.

My fingers brushing over the cold metal handle wrapping around it. I swing the door open and look around the front yard, down the street. My eyes flit over every detail, looking for someone or something out of the ordinary. It's not until I look down that I notice it. A shrill scream departs my body and I slam the door closed. My hands shake as I work to spin the lock and secure it. I blink a few times, before finally brushing the curtains aside to look out the long floor to ceiling window. I didn't want to believe it, but there is absolutely no mistaking what is laying on my front porch.

Stiff, lifeless, and somewhat bloody, a large black raven smack dab in the middle of my front mat. If I were to take one singular step out the door, my foot would no doubt land against its dead body. *Why is this happening? Who would do such a thing?* My mind races with question after question, each one leading me to the same answer. It's the masked man. My masked stalker. The one and only person I can't get out of my mind. I've been thinking about him and all our encounters, but especially the time at the gym. Blood pumps through my veins mixed with fear and adrenaline as my heartbeat races. *Am I afraid of him? Or am I secretly hoping he might show up to ravish my body again?* My pussy tingles at the thought of him, re-membering once again how good it felt and how thrilling it was to be fucked by a masked psychopath.

I squeeze my eyes shut, angry with myself and these thoughts of being with another man. My man, my sweet, thoughtful boyfriend, who might be the most amazing human in the world went through great lengths to make sure I had an amazing Halloween day while he is away working to support us both right now, and here I am fantasizing about cheating on him with a mysterious masked man. Damn, I'm just the fucking worst. The tear drops drip down my face and fall from my chin onto my T-shirt, and I hastily wipe and dab at them. I shouldn't feel guilty, I tried to tell him, but he doesn't believe me. Maybe I need to try to tell him again, or perhaps I should just force myself never to think about him again. *Can I do that?* I wonder. My mind immediately retreats to think about his piercing and how much I've always wanted to have sex with somebody that has their dick pierced. I've begged and pleaded with my boyfriend to do it. I even got my nipples pierced as a trade for him, but he completely chickened out and refused to follow through.

My phone chimes, pulling me from my thoughts. It's him which only makes me feel worse. His text says he's just checking on me. I decide to lie and say I'm fine, then ask if he'll be home soon. I wait for him to reply, but he doesn't. Or at least not right away. I convince myself to make something for lunch and end up curled up on the living room couch in what has become my favorite afternoon spot. Feeling restless and unnerved, I remember the tea in the boo basket is calm down tea and decide to brew a cup. I could use some rest, especially if I want to stay up late enough and try to satisfy my body's cravings to be stuffed full of a nice fat cock.

"Cheers," I say to myself, holding up a Halloween mug filled with piping hot relaxation tea. "Bottoms up, and I better take the best nap ever." I tip the contents into my mouth and have to choke it down. I always forget how much I don't like tea. Yuck. I feel my stomach give a lurch but manage to keep myself from vomiting its contents. I grab my brand new boo blanket then snuggle in for a movie and a nap. The sunset will wake me later, like it does everyday around four o'clock.

2:00 PM

Chapter Sixteen

Mask

Before heading around back, I open the camera app from my phone and disable the doorbell feed. There's one thing I need to take care of first. Holding an old shoe box, I climb the front steps and scoop the dead raven back inside of it. In its place, I leave a mask that looks just like the one I've been wearing to disguise my identity. I got the idea to leave her a bird like this from some of the books I've watched her read while she touches herself at night. Last night I wrestled the dead raven from the neighborhood tabby. It was a lucky coincidence our paths crossed. I was standing in the alley, trying to figure out how to find a dead black bird and he came meandering by with it dangling from his mouth. He even chewed on one side, making it nice and bloody, perfect for the front step. I slip the lid gingerly over the shoebox grave so I can dispose of it in a trash can that stands at attention in the alley, like a soldier waiting for his orders to make the evidence disappear. The mask on the step makes the scene picturesque, a true work of art. Adrenaline works its way through my system at the thought of her finding the mask. I can't wait to see the tortured look on her face later.

Satisfied with my display, I creep around back to sneak into the basement side window, but first I slip into the garage spying on her from my perch inside. My binoculars provide me with an up-close experience. I watch through them as she drinks a cup of tea. I tucked the relaxing tea into her boo basket earlier, before she woke up. It's supposed to help you fall asleep and stay asleep, according to the box the tea bags arrived in. My lip curls up into a villainous smirk. Soon she'll be out like a corpse and I can finish up the rest of my plans for tonight. I've been anxiously waiting for this day, counting down the hours until I can slide into her slick wet pussy; feeling it clench around me tight and hot, while I listen to her moaning everything I tell her to. My thoughts wander to my lava-coated playground, obsessing over Amanda as I greedily wait for my opportunity to slip back inside the house undetected. It's not long before she falls asleep watching her movie. After fifteen minutes of grueling waiting, I climb through the window, then creep quietly into the basement.

Inside, I retrieve the backpack I left the other day from the crawl space and stealthily tiptoe up the basement steps. Before I open the door, I slip the mask into place. If I'm caught, I don't want her to see my face, not yet at least.

Now that I have free rein of the house for a few hours, I'll be making myself nice and cozy. Upstairs, I stop in the kitchen first to refill the water in the vase with the flowers I sent her. They sit slowly dying on the kitchen counter, as the life seeps from them. It makes me excited to think I've already squirmed my way into her thoughts so many times.

Before I tossed the raven from this morning in the trash, I plucked a decent amount of bloody feathers from its dead body, stuffed them in a ziplock bag, and tucked them in my pocket. I pull the bag out and retrieve a few feathers. I leave two on the counter and balance the third on one of the sunflowers. Looking at my handiwork has me wishing I'd kept the bird for a second appearance. I check the running stopwatch timer I set on my watch as I walk to the other room to check on my snoozing little masterpiece. Her chest rises and falls steadily. She looks so peaceful while she sleeps. Her face is no longer contorted with fear like it was when she raced down the street away from me the last time we were together. *It's too bad,* I think with a sigh. I wouldn't have minded fingering her until she came. The little slut must be exhausted from her scare this morning. Combined with her pleasure session the other night and recent relapse with late-night reading, it's easy to see why she needs a nap. I want her to be nice and refreshed. As tempting as it might be to rush my plan and take her now, I fight hard to resist the urges pulsing through my body. It's so tempting to fuck her while she sleeps, but I want to hear her voice, and watch her body tremble with a mix of fear and desire again as she's overcome with a flood of emotions.

"Maybe in a little while, you tease," I whisper to her, blowing a kiss, and heading to the entryway, wandering upstairs next.

It's going to be me and her all alone for the rest of the day. I can't fucking wait to follow her every move from my cameras while I hide away in the upstairs home office where I plan to set up for the night. Thanks to her voracious reading, I've come up with plenty of ideas. Waiting until after it gets dark will be half the fun. When the lights go out and the trick-or-treaters have had their fill, I'll be ready for my turn. Once I have her nice and scared, that's when things are going to really heat up. I lick my lips, thinking about it again. She's so fucking sexy and tonight I'll have her all to myself.

Upstairs, I drop my bag off in the office where I'll be waiting for her tonight and grab the few items out of it I will need. Then I slink to her bedroom to leave a sexy lingerie set with a note on the bed for her. I even leave her a book based on some of her current reads. Since she's a bit of a bookstagrammer in her free time, it was easy to find her wishlist. There's another note hidden inside of the book. The look on her face when she gets to that part is going to be worth all the waiting and planning. I smile to myself, thinking about what it says. Working my way back downstairs, I lay a mixture of the bloody feathers I plucked from the raven with fake black feathers on the stairs in clumps. Thanks to the craft store, those feathers were easy to acquire and didn't require any plucking. I put a few finishing touches on the stairs, then creep back to the main floor to check on my sweet, innocent sleeping beauty.

Right where I left you is all I can think as my eyes sweep over her. It's so hard to fight the urge not to go to her. I want to but I can't bring myself to do it. Instead, I slide silently into a chair to watch her sleep a while longer. Of course, I should have known watching could never satisfy me, not with such a perfect victim unaware of the predator lurking inside her home. Desperation overwhelms my senses as I continue to study her supple lips. Lips that are plump and perfect, just begging to wrap around my needy cock while I ram it deep into her throat. It has me daydreaming about how good she sucked it last time. She enjoyed playing with me, using her tongue to lick over my piercing seductively. I bite back a moan as my cock twitches in agreement. I allow my fantasy to continue playing out, imagining the feel of her tight cunt squeezing around my throbbing cock. All the while, my fingers grasp her dainty neck, depriving her of oxygen as I take what I've been craving for so long. I want to ram my dick inside of her repeatedly until her eyes fill with tears and she's begging me to stop.

I'm no longer able to resist the urge to touch her. I want to feel her skin against my own. The movie is almost over. Instinctively, I look down to check the running stopwatch.

The clock is ticking away, bringing us closer to our night together. I'll have to force myself to retreat upstairs. The obsession with running my hands over the curves of her breasts consumes my thoughts. I get up from the chair, standing over Amanda to admire her for just one last moment. Despite myself, I allow my fingers to reach out and play in her hair. They're out of control, unleashed with a plan of their own. They lightly run down the length of her body, taking extra care to linger on her thigh. My fingers are so tempted to steal a touch. I have no self-control. My hands continue to roam on their own. They slide up the opening of her sweat shorts and beneath her panties. One of my fingertips rubs against her pussy, just a small touch at first, but then I get carried away. Stroking through her folds while she slumbers on the couch. The little slut is so deprived of a man's attention she moans softly in her sleep, flexing her hips, trying to find the friction my fingertip created. Unable to deny her, my finger travels against her a few more times before it slips inside of her. She gasps in her sleep. It's so hard to walk away when she's already begging for my touch, responding to me with so much need. Amanda moans again as I slip another finger in, curling it as I pump in and out slowly. She stirs and her eyelashes flutter. I know it's time to retreat. Staying only puts me at risk of her catching me before I am ready for her to know I'm here. I pull the two fingers I slipped inside of her from her wet cunt, bringing them to my mouth and sucking her savory juices from each finger. *That pussy is going to taste delicious later tonight,* I think as I slip away to retire to my hiding spot upstairs. I know her tendencies like the back of my hand and she never once in all my weeks of watching her has entered the other bedroom where an office sits untouched most days. Tonight, it will be my secret sanctuary.

5:00 PM

Chapter Seventeen

Amanda

The silence of the TV, and glow from the setting sun wake me like they have almost every day since I took my leave from work. I yawn then stretch, kicking the blanket off myself and returning it to the bin beside the couch. The house is quiet, and the sun beams in through the window like it's informing me Halloween is about to begin. I check my phone. There's a missed text from my boyfriend telling me he got pulled into an emergency meeting for the event tonight and won't be on time. I'm not surprised. In fact, I don't even know why I got my hopes up thinking he would actually spend my favorite holiday with me.

It's probably unfair of me to be upset with him. He worked really hard for the opportunity to become a partner at work. I know he wants to prove he can support us both. If I'm being honest with myself, I'm considering his offer but he needs to understand, depending on another person like that when we aren't even married makes me uncomfortable. I've given it a lot of thought and I'm still considering moving part time as a compromise, or taking up Erica on her business opportunity.

It's complicated though and our perfect, sexless relationship is confusing the fuck out of me. Everything feels so hot and cold right now. It has me second guessing if our relationship can handle these changes. Honestly, my recent behavior has me questioning my morals. I can't think about this right now. A glance out the back door alerts me it's getting dark out. I have plenty of things I would rather do to pass the time waiting for him. Which includes setting out the bowl of candy. Fuck! The dead bird on the front porch. I'm going to have to move it off the welcome mat. Ugh. I trudge groggily to the kitchen to retrieve the bowl of candy and look for something to move the dead body. I grab the broom from the pantry first, then reach for the bowl on the countertop. As I pick up the bowl from the counter, I notice bloody black feathers strewn next to the vase of sunflowers. My pulse quickens and my eyes dart around everywhere. *What the fuck is going on? Is he creeping around the house, messing with me? Shut the fuck up, Amanda. All the alarms are set and he would have to break inside. Don't do this.* My mind is racing.

No matter what, I'm going to have to work up enough courage to scoop the bird into the bushes so the trick-or-treaters don't see it. I really, really don't want to. Maybe we can just skip the festivities this year. Ugh, I know I can't actually do that. I take a deep breath and with the bowl full of candy, I scurry to the front door, ready to bravely push the dead bird into the bushes with the broom. To my surprise, when I open the front door, the bird is gone. In its place is a black mask with neon colored threading. I kick it to the side right into the bushes, then inspect the porch quickly. There's no sign of the bird anywhere, and the neighbors probably think I'm insane. Especially after my mad dash inside this morning and the crazy kicking going on right now. I set down the bowl and rush back inside, trying to avoid drawing any more atten-tion to myself. I slam the door shut behind me, locking it, and squeeze my eyes closed, falling against the wall. This is all too much. I should have spent the day with Erica instead of home alone. She was doing the trick-or-treat street at the shop tonight for the neighborhood kids. I've tried calling the police, but it's useless. No one believes me about anything that's been happening. My fear consumes me, making it hard to focus. I take a few deep breaths, trying to calm my nerves. When I open my eyes, they land on the stairs. I scream, bolting for the bedroom. The stairs are covered in black feathers, just like the bird. I take them two or three at a time, trying my best not to land on any, then flying down the hall to the perceived safety of my bedroom.

My heart is beating out of my chest, but it doesn't stop me from noticing something out of place. On the bed is a gift bag with a card. I cautiously empty the contents to find some sexy lingerie and a book. I open the card. Inside is another note. The handwriting matches the note on the flowers earlier. It reads, *"Put this on and enjoy the book."*

I'm not sure what to think. *Who is this from? It has to be from my man, obviously. Or am I losing my mind?* Once again, my thoughts overwhelm my senses. I stand with my back against the locked bedroom door, arms crossed, glaring at the gift bag, contemplating whether or not to put the lingerie on. A glance at the time on my phone lets me know it's late enough. I can get away with a call to check on him. Trying my best to take deep breaths and remain calm, I tap on his phone number and wait for the line to ring. He answers right away, catching me off-guard.

"Hey, babe." He's nonchalant, like nothing is wrong. "I'm just wrapping up here."

"Okay," I squeak out, fighting back the tears.

"Is everything alright?" He asks, immediately concerned.

"I'm just having a weird night. That's all," I confess.

"I'll be home soon, baby. Why don't you take a shower and read for a little while? Enjoy yourself and I'll be home before you know it. I'm sorry I am running late."

I nod my reply as if he can see me through the phone, then recover. "Okay, I guess I can take a shower while I wait for you to get here. It's too bad you aren't here to take one with me."

He giggles uncomfortably. "See you soon, love you," he says sweetly.

"Love you too," I reply before hanging up.

Hearing his voice made me feel a lot better, and knowing he's on his way home soon calms my nerves. Based on his suggestion that I take a shower and read a book, I think it's safe to assume the gifts are from him. I mean, obviously, who else can it realistically be? There's no way anyone got in without setting off the alarm. No one else has access to my wishlist to know this book is on there. I grab the lingerie, taking it with me to the bathroom and turn on the shower. Water always helps me feel better. It's just what I need to relax and focus. Tonight is going to be much needed. I'm literally counting down the minutes until date night is going to begin. All my sexual frustration is pent up and I'm ready to lose control.

7:00 PM

Chapter Eighteen

Mask

This office is the perfect hiding space. I pull two tablets from my backpack and set up the live camera feed. In the walls, I hear the water turn on. My lips curl up in a dubious smile. She's in the shower, which means it's time for me to enjoy the show from my front-row seat. I've always wanted to watch her up close and in person instead of from my hideout in the alley. It's such a convenient coincidence, and I'm not the least bit disappointed in my role. My hand runs over my cock slowly. I'm going to give her a little scare. I need a little something to get me all worked up. It won't take much to get her heart racing and blood pumping. Terrifying her turns me on more than I expected it to. One time was all it took to leave me craving more. I need that sweet little pussy to be burning hot from the adrenaline pulsing through her veins. Overcome and consumed by my desire to feel her wrapped around me, I sneak out of the office, down the hall, and into Amanda's room. From there, I watch her waiting patiently for the ideal opportunity to slip around the corner and into her closet.

My mask is in place: I made sure of that before I left the safety of the office hideout. The eye holes aren't big enough for me to watch her in the water as it washes over her. I need a better view, and the seconds feel like minutes waiting for her to relax. Finally, she dips her head into the water, closing her eyes and allowing it to drip down her face. I take advantage of this opportunity to glide from her bedroom into the closet undetected while she shampoos her hair. The delicious aroma of her soap fills the bathroom, damn near driving me far enough over the edge to spring from my hiding spot, slamming her against the tile of the shower. Then fucking her while the burning hot water falls on our bodies. I want to fuck her so hard the tile cracks from the impact of my thrusts. The thought of pounding the fuck out of her is all I needed to get me going. I watch Amanda through the crack between the second door in her closet and the doorframe, leaning against the massive wall for support. I have an up-close view right into the bathroom, maybe three feet from the shower. It really is too easy to lose myself watching her. My mouth waters at the mere sight of her naked body. Water droplets roll down her supple skin, between her breasts, lower and lower. My cock is hard, begging to be unleashed while my eyes eagerly follow the trail the water leaves as it runs across her pussy. She's a fucking goddess, my irresistible little masterpiece. I can't control myself. I hold my throbbing cock firmly as she rinses the soap from all the curves and crevices. Until suddenly I realize as she turns the water off that I've missed my opportunity to escape. Too enthralled in the hypnotizing patterns of the water streaking across her skin, I left myself vulnerable and potentially exposed. When she bends over to wrap a towel around her wet hair, I reach outside the closet door for the bathroom light switch and flip it off. She screams, igniting my senses. I don't want to go. I want to stay and play with her. Despite that, I use the cover of the darkness to slip out of my hiding spot, ducking back into the actual bedroom, leaving her alone in the bathroom, searching the wall for the light switch. I peek around the corner, certain

I'll find her staring right at the glowing neon threads of my mask. Instead, I can see her silhouette in the shower. She's clutching at her towel, reaching for the switch, trying to feel along that part of the wall. Having narrowly escaped being caught, it's my cue to retreat to the office sanctuary, where my presence remains unknown.

Back inside the office, I return to viewing the camera feed on my tablets. I'm only disappointed I couldn't stay to enjoy watching her longer. She's still standing in the bathroom. Her body trembles as her eyes dart across every surface. She's too terrified to move. I wish she would drop the towel she's clutching. There's also the lingerie waiting for her on the bed. I wouldn't mind watching her dress in it. I picked the black lacy number out for our special night together. After a few minutes of shock, Amanda appears to be trying to calm herself down. If I could hear inside her head, I'm sure she would be suggesting she's lost her mind and acting silly. As hard as it is to wait, I resist the urge to scare her anymore for now. It will be more fun in the long run to allow her to feel a false sense of security before I rip it away. After another ten minutes, she leaves the bathroom uneasily. I perk up in my chair. She's pulling the lingerie from the bag. I watch with my eyes glued to the screen as she dresses in the black lace bodysuit. It hugs her curves in all the right places, highlighting all the best features as it clings to her body. Her nipples are hard from the chill in the air. They press against the lace, begging for the warmth of my mouth. My tongue wets my lips as I fantasize about licking over each one, feeling their arousal against my hungry tongue. My imagination is dying to act out the scene with her.

She disappears for a moment and returns wearing a soft silk robe. The filthy little tease couldn't give me the satisfaction of laying there practically naked, reading the dirty Halloween romance I left for her. I'll be sure to punish her for it later. I lean back in the leather office chair and watch as she settles in to read. Mmmmm, I can't wait to see her reaction when she gets to my note.

It takes her just under twenty minutes to reach my note and when she does, she immediately slams the book down, looking around the room nervously. I laugh. It's time. It's finally fucking time. I let her panic for a moment longer, then using an app to scramble my number, and flipping on the voice disguiser in my mask, I call her.

She lets it ring to voicemail, so I call a second time. This time she answers.

"Hello," she says nervously.

"Hello, Masterpiece." I rasp.

"What do you want? Why are you doing this?" Her voice cracks.

"I want to play a game, Amanda." I stroke my cock as we speak.

"Leave me alone," she shouts.

"I only want to ask you a few questions," I reply, knowing at any moment she can hang up on me and ruin all my fun.

"No!" she yells.

I ignore her, asking anyway. "Do you like scary books, Amanda?"

The line is quiet. She says nothing for a moment, creating a long pause. "Yes," she answers.

"Let's play a game. I'll tell you about one of the books you've read this month and you guess which one I am describing."

"I don't want to play. Leave me alone. The doors are locked, so are the windows, and my boyfriend is on his way home," she quips.

"What if I'm inside the house, Amanda?" I ask, taunting her.

"You can't be inside the house because I set the security system, asshole." She snaps.

"You mean the security system that I just disabled?" I flip the system from armed to unarmed with the app on my phone.

"Fuck you, asshole. My boyfriend will be home any minute," she yells.

"Oh, tsk tsk tsk, Amanda. A pretty girl like you shouldn't lie. We both know he's never going to make it home unless you cooperate." I pause dramatically for a minute. "Oops, I guess only I knew that. Oh well, now we both know, so how about that game?" My voice is dripping with danger.

On the other end of the phone line, I can hear her breathing intensify. She's probably checking the app right now and finding it disabled. I wait to hear her scream, but nothing happens.

"What's wrong, Amanda, cat got your tongue?" I laugh.

"Fuck you, I'm calling the police," she shouts.

"Oh you will fuck me, don't you worry, little slut. I've been watching you and I know about all those nights alone with your toys. Don't you remember, I know all about what a needy little whore you are—or have you already forgotten the night we spent together at the gym?"

The line goes dead. Beneath the mask, I smile. It's finally fucking time.

8:00 PM

Chapter Nineteen

Amanda

I'm paralyzed with fear, but only for a moment. The world is moving in slow motion until the initial wave of crippling terror passes, and the world speeds up around me again. I lunge for the bedroom door in an attempt to lock myself inside. I'm not fast enough. The realization hits me just as I reach the door handle and see the glow of the mask. Two X's mark the spot where the eyes should be. The tall, rugged figure fills the door frame once more. Except we aren't at the gym this time, and there's no chance of anyone coming to rescue me. He's wearing his signature outfit: a pair of gray sweatpants and a black zip-up hoodie. His muscular body is so close I can reach out and touch it. Part of me wants to.

I might be sexually frustrated, but I'm not stupid. Instinctively, I try to slam the door in his face, but his arm flies out, stopping it. He's not even trying to use his strength against me, but the door kicks back, sending me falling to the ground from the force. As soon as I recover, I crawl away from him. It doesn't matter. I look over my shoulder and see him step into my bedroom, locking the door behind him as he does.

"Mmmmm," the masked man rumbles. "You're crawling in the wrong direction, Amanda, but I'll allow it for now, since I have a damn good view."

I shift myself around, trying to conceal my revealing lingerie.

"Don't hide, Masterpiece. I want to admire the way you look in my gift. Do you like it? I sent it for our special night together." He takes a step toward me and I freeze.

"Oh, you didn't think that was from me?" He chuckles, towering over me he reaches down, pulling my robe off my shoulder and sliding one finger beneath the lingerie strap. He pulls up, snapping it against my skin.

His laugh gives me the chills and I shudder.

"I like what I see. Why don't you spread those legs open so I can get a better look at you? It's not the same watching from my binoculars." His hand lands on my knee and slides slowly up my thigh.

I'm trembling, but I snap my legs closed tight, desperate not to give this intruder what he wants. "You really should leave. My boyfriend is going to be home any minute. Just leave and we can forget this ever even happened." I reply, staring him down, trying to appear tougher than I really am.

He snickers. "What a brave little play toy you are. Something tells me he's preoccupied. I'm sorry, Amanda, he's going to miss your date."

"No, you're wrong," I scream, scooting away from him, scanning the room for an escape.

"Shame on you, little slut, trying to get away from me like that. I think I need to teach you a lesson," he says, taking another step closer, closing the distance between us again.

The moment his body hovers over me this time, everything changes. It all becomes so real. *How are the pages of my horror stories coming to life? This shouldn't be happening, it can't be happening,* I'm in denial. Yet it is happening. I don't want to take my eyes off of him, but I roll onto my knees anyway trying to escape out of his reach.

In a split second, I feel his fingers wrap around my ankle as he latches onto it and pulls me back to the middle of the room.

"And just where do you think you're going?" He snarls, landing on top of me and pinning my arms above my head in one smooth motion.

I scream. There's nothing left to do. He's so much stronger than I am. I don't stand a chance against him.

"That's a good girl. Go ahead and struggle. The way you scream while your hips thrust into me only turns me on more," he growls, leaning in close against my ear.

His free hand strokes my hair, and then runs down my chin, until he's tipping it to look him square on. "If you're a good girl, Amanda, we can both enjoy ourselves tonight."

"I don't want to enjoy myself with you," I shout.

"Oh, not with me? Then perhaps by yourself. Shall I fetch your toy from the drawer? I would love to watch you play with yourself up-close instead of from the alley." He laughs a sinister laugh and runs his hand down my body to cup my breast.

"Fucking creep! I knew someone was watching me. Get off!" I scream, trying to wiggle myself free, but it's no use. He has me pinned.

"That's enough of that," he snarls, putting his hand over my mouth so that the edge of his palm is cutting off my ability to breathe through my nose.

I struggle against him, trying to gasp for air.

"No more screaming," he demands. "Now take this off," he plucks at my robe. "Or I'll ruin it, and I know how excited you were to save it for such a special night."

He releases my arms and uses his other hand to slide beneath my robe, slipping his hand beneath to cup my breast before pulling the tie, and ripping it off my body. I don't make it easy for him, so he grabs me by the throat and uses only his pointer finger to draw my jawline so that I'm forced to stare at the mask.

"Fuck you, don't touch me anymore." That's a lie. My body is melting for him, enjoying every rough touch. I don't want him to stop. I want him to take this so much further. My pussy aches to be filled and my nipples are peaked and hard, waiting for him.

"I'll touch whatever I want, and you're going to do exactly what I tell you to, if you want to see that boyfriend of yours again."

I gulp, knowing he can feel how hard I'm swallowing as he makes his demands known, all the while squeezing my throat to let me know he can snap it in a heartbeat.

I go limp, willingly submitting my body to him, letting him know I'll allow him to take whatever he wants from me.

He slams my knees apart, then drags his fingers through my wetness, slipping them beneath the mask to suck my juices off.

"You're so fucking delicious, Amanda. Do you know how bad I want to taste you? Do you know how much I want you to cum all over my tongue so I can lick it all up?"

I don't answer. My brain cannot process anything but how fucking hot his words are. I shouldn't be attracted to my stalker like this. I shouldn't want him to take me like this, but I do.

"That's a good little slut," he moans, giving my nipple a pinch when my back arches. "I'm going to let you go, because if you run, I'm going to chase you; and if I chase you, I might just carve up that pretty little face of yours to teach you a lesson." He pulls out a large pocket knife and flips it open. "You're going to show me how much you want me to let you live. Get your ass on that bed. Now!" He shouts, releasing me.

9:00 PM

Chapter Twenty

Mask

She's so fucking obedient. She'll do anything I tell her to because she wants me just as bad as I want her. It's driving me absolutely wild. My cock is hard and ready to slam deep inside of her, but I haven't even gotten to the fun part yet. I keep my eyes locked on hers beneath the mask. I know her well enough to know not to take my eyes off of her. From the bedside drawer, I pull out her toy, turn it on, and hand it to her.

"I want to watch you cum. Spread those legs open so I can watch." I use the flat side of my blade to press her legs open. "That's better. It's just like all the other nights."

I use the knife to cut the bikini string on her lingerie. I hope she knows better than to defy me. Her breathing is heavy as she dips her toy between her legs and drags it across her pussy. After a few passes, her clit glistens with cum while she watches me, waiting for my approval. It's all so fucking sexy. I drag the handle of my knife against her supple skin, holding it dangerously by the blade without a care in the world. Her breathing is short and ragged. The hilt glides across her clit and down to drift inside of her. I fuck her with the handle of my knife until she comes, soaking my hand. It's more than I can take. I pull the handle out of her soaking wet pussy.

"Play with yourself again," I demand, folding the knife closed, setting it on the edge of the bed and dropping my pants to the floor. I step out of them. My hand finds my cock and I slather my dick with her cum. I'm stroking myself while I watch her, imagining the feel of her pussy clenching around me, pulsing as she soaks every inch of my dick.

"My poor little slut, do you need my dick to fill you up?"

Her breath hitches as her legs tremble from the buzzing sensation of the silicone against her sensitive pussy. She may not say it, but I know my masterpiece wants to feel this enormous cock inside her.

"Use your words and answer me, little whore. Do you want my cock inside of you, filling you up inch by fucking inch, stretching that tight little pussy of yours out?" I growl.

She still doesn't answer me.

"Answer me, damn it," I snarl, annoyed by her silence.

"Yes," she whispers.

"I can't hear you," I snap.

"Yes," she says louder, looking away from me.

I'm straddling her in an instant, grabbing her by the chin. "Eyes on mine. Yes, what?" I seethe, my masked face inches from her lips.

I release my cock and grab her by the hair. I said, "Yes, what, little slut?"

"Yes, Mask Daddy," she sulks.

"That's my girl," I praise her. "And good girls get rewarded." I reach between her legs, pumping my fingers in and out of her pussy until she's clenching around me. "Cum for me, Masterpiece. Such a naughty little whore."

I sit back on my knees, admiring her. I've been waiting weeks for this. She's panting. Her body no longer responds in fear, instead it craves me. It calls to me, begging me to ravish her. But first I want to feel her lips on my cock, sucking me like the filthy little whore she is. I crawl beside her, tracing my fingertips up the slopes of her breasts and swirl them around her hard nipple.

"You're going to suck my dick before I fuck you. We are going to play by my rules. Do you understand?" I ask.

"What are your rules?"

"You bite me and your man doesn't survive the night."

Tears well in her eyes, and she nods her head in agreement.

"I can't hear you, Amanda. What do you say?"

"Yes, Mask Daddy." She glares at me.

I grip the base of my cock, dangling it in front of her face, but she doesn't make a move. "Open your mouth," I say, reaching for the knife and slipping the blade against her throat when she decides to be defiant.

Her pretty lips open wide and swallow my cock. I'm thrusting into her throat as my fingers work her into another release. She feels so fucking good, the way she explodes all over me. I fuck her mouth harder and growl, "Swallow my cum, Masterpiece. That's my girl."

When she does, I moan, then hook her by the leg and flip her over in a sexy maneuver. "You're going to take this big dick now, little slut. You're going to take it until you can't cum anymore." I grab her by the hair and shove her face into the pillow.

I position myself behind her and slide inside. Her core is slick and hot. I have no issues pushing deeper and deeper inside of her until I feel her enveloping me. She feels so fucking amazing. It's everything I've been thinking about. My cock grows at least another inch inside her as I pull out just a little, then slam inside that tight, wet pussy. She drenches me uncontrollably and cums hard. It makes me moan. I fuck her hard like this while gripping her by the hair and shoving her face into the pillows. She can't help it the way she screams for me.

"I want to hear you beg for me, Amanda."

"Please," she whimpers.

She's got me so close to a release as I pound into her, unrelenting. I drag my blade down her back, applying just enough pressure to break the surface of her skin. She hisses as the blood dibbles to the surface.

"Sunflower," she gasps. "I get it. The metaphors, the subtle hints, the nickname. We need a safe word."

Ignoring her, I reach down to stroke her swollen clit. "There are no safe words, Sunflower."

I drag my hand down her back, smearing the blood, then rub it across her pussy. Her clit is so fucking hard. It sends her over the edge. At last she's thrusting against me, fucking me back while she chases her release.

I rasp in her ear. "That's my girl. That's my good little slut. She just needed to be filled, didn't she? Be a good girl and cum on me, Amanda? I want to feel you squeezing around my big dick. It's so fucking hard for you. All from watching you play with yourself. All for you, my little masterpiece."

She throws her head back moaning and I pull her hair tighter.

"Fuck me harder, little slut. That's it, there's the orgasm you've been so naughty for," I groan. She slips rhythmically on and off of my cock, bringing me closer to my release. I explode into her and shudder as my cum fills her so full, it's leaking back out.

She trembles as she orgasms coming with me. She did everything I told her to, hoping I would allow her to live. It's time for the big reveal and I think she might be disappointed. It's too late now not to go through with it. I've spent the last thirty-one days making sure this moment is perfect. I pull my dick from her, leaving her laying face down. She rolls over onto her back and takes advantage of my moment of weakness. As I bend down to pick up my sweatpants, she reaches for my mask.

Her fingers hook beneath it, sliding it in slow motion over my chin, then my lips. She lifts it past my nose and then rips it from my face completely. To her surprise, I don't pull away, or try to prevent her from figuring out my identity. The mask falls from my face in one fluid motion.

Amanda gasps in surprise as she stares back at me. A devious smile spreads from ear to ear across my face.

"What the fuck?" She says angrily, her body shaking with rage. "It's you!"

She looks at me confused, then fires off questions in a rapid succession. "Is this why you've been working late? Why you didn't answer when I texted you?"

"Guity," I reply with a grin.

She points to the healed piercing just below the head of my dick. "Is this why we haven't had sex in weeks?"

"Happy Halloween, Amanda," I rasp, leaning in to kiss her cheek. "I wanted to surprise you by playing out one of your dirty book scenes. I picked up one of your copies a few weeks ago for research and decided I could recreate it."

Blown away by my thoughtfulness, she smiles. "I'm speechless. I can't believe you did this for me."

"I felt bad for chickening out, but that's not the only reason." I confess.

"Were you following me around too?" She asks.

"Guilty," I answer, leaning over to kiss her on the forehead. "Didn't you know it was me?" I ask, raising a brow.

"That's so fucking hot," she moans, reaching for me to wrap her arms around my neck.

I lean into her embrace, climbing on top of her, pressing us back into our pillows, and kiss her lightly.

When I pull away. A serious look adorns her face, like she's offended I left her.

"There's one more thing," I whisper. "I wanted this to be perfect for you."

Sliding off of her and over to my side of the bed. I reach into my bedside table and retrieve a small black box. Sitting on one knee, I hand the box to Amanda. She has fresh tears running down her face.

"Amanda, will you please quit your job and marry me?" I ask.

"You did all this just to propose to me? You pierced your dick? You read my books? You stalked me?" She shakes her head in disbelief.

"All for you, my love—"

"Masterpiece." She corrects me.

"All for you, Masterpiece." I say.

She smiles, wiping her tears from her cheeks. "Yes!" She squeals, snuggling into me. "How could I say no to a man who will do literally anything for me?"

I shrug my shoulders. "Do you want me to put it on for you?"

She nods, handing me the box back. I slip the sparkling ring from the box before kissing her hand lightly and slide it on to her finger. "I love you, Amanda."

THE END

EPILOGUE

Amanda

I quit my job to live out role playing all my fantasies with the perfect mask daddy.

DID YOU ENJOY MASK DADDY?

If you enjoyed this masked stalker romance keep reading

with:

Book 2: Hunted For Christmas

Book 3: Chasing An Obsession

About Des Sweet

Des writes deliciously dark romances in the contemporary and paranormal genres. Her books contain dark themes and characters in varying shades of morally gray. She's a sucker for the bad guy getting the girl. Demons, creatures, unalivers, stalkers, and mafia men frequent her pages. Her books might leave you with a new kink, or obsessing over a filthy mouthed book boyfriend. Popular tropes she enjoys writing include: enemies to lovers, forced proximity, and torture, in many different forms. Her name may sound sweet, but there's nothing sweet about the things she's writing, unless it's her morally gray contemporary romance line.

Looking for more content?

Follow Des on REAM for FREE or become a member: https://reamstories.com/dessweet

Interested in joining her Newsletter for first peeks, and exciting new releases or following her on social media? Join her reader group on Facebook, find out how to order signed copies, chat about her books, meet other readers, and stay up to date on all the details for upcoming projects. You can find everything you need in one convenient place: https://linktr.ee/DesSweetWrites

ALSO BY DES SWEET

Kindle/Kindle Unlimited:

Chasing An Obsession

Hunted for Christmas

Underneath the Mask

The Birthday Buy

Baby, It Snowed Outside

Revenge Body

B is for Bonnie

Ream / Patreon Subscription Stories:

Heathens of Hawthorn Hill (Patreon only)

Home Run Hunk

Stolen Kisses

Ringmaster

Carnival of Souls